LADY IN LILAC

LADY IN LILAC

SUSANNAH SHANE

COACHWHIP PUBLICATIONS

GREENVILLE, OHIO

About the Author

Susannah Shane was the pseudonym for Harriette Cora Ashbrook (1898-1946), originally hailing from Mitchell, Nebraska. Ashbrook wrote six mystery novels as Shane and seven under her own name. Reviewers note that her mysteries are well-plotted with enjoyable characters and a keen sense of humor.

Graduating from the University of Nebraska, Ashbrook started out as a newspaper woman. She worked in Lincoln (NE), Calgary, the west coast, Boston, and New York, writing her way up to features. She also authored numerous popular magazine articles and became a publicity agent for Coward-McCann book publishers. Ashbrook said that she was first inspired to write a mystery when, while proof-reading a detective story so bad, she said to herself, "If this is a BOOK, then I, too, can do one!"

Living for some time in New York, she claimed that the bustle and activity of a large city made it much easier to write a mystery, but illness forced her to return to Nebraska, where she finished her later books starting with *Murder Comes Back* in 1940. ('. . . a breezy, cussy yarn with accent on flippancy. It's recommended for mystery novel fans whose tastes are jaded from too many corpses on blood stained carpets and who want their stories spiced with the ginger which H. Ashbrook deftly sprinkles.') It was after moving home to Nebraska that she started using the pseudonym Susannah Shane, first using it to win the $1,000 Red Badge Mystery Prize with *Lady in Lilac*. She died at her parents' home in Mitchell, NE, in 1946, leaving behind a full legacy of enjoyable detective novels which deserve a second look by mystery readers today.

Harriette Ashbrook

Lady in Lilac

1

It was hot. Too hot, with waves of June heat rising from the sultry asphalt to meet the sweating blanket of mist that seemed to press down from the smoke-laden sky.

The small, cramped bedroom directly beneath the baking roof of the old brownstone front was hotter still, and there was no breath of air stirring through the one window that looked out upon acres of other brownstone fronts and baking roofs.

The girl looked tired and wilted, but there was a rueful, half-humorous twist to her lips as she looked at the three discouraging objects on the dresser before her.

A single half dollar.

A note penciled on cheap tablet paper. "Miss—You're three weeks behind now and I'll have to have my rent by tomorrow morning or else have the room.—Mrs. Anna Price."

She picked up the third object, a small, white card.

"Personnel Division, JASON RESTAURANTS, Inc. This is to certify that Helen Varney has been approved by the Personnel Division as a waitress and placed at the disposal of Unit 7—Sixth Avenue. M. B. Crotty, Personnel Director." The name, Helen Varney, the words "waitress" and "Unit 7—Sixth Avenue" were filled in with ink on the printed form.

She looked at it a long time and then sighed. The rueful smile grew more rueful, but she shrugged her shoulders philosophically as she scooped up the half dollar, the note from Mrs. Anna Price and the card from M. B. Crotty and stuffed them into her handbag.

She shook her heavy, dark hair back from her forehead and pressed her hands against hot temples. At the window she leaned over the sill, searching vainly for a vagrant stirring of air. She gazed out over the rooftops. There was no moon. There was no balcony. There was no passionate, palpitant lover waiting below. But suddenly she stretched out her arms and her voice came deep and lovely with a touch of laughter lilting through the immortal words:

> "O Romeo, Romeo!
> Wherefore art thou Romeo?
> Deny thy father and refuse thy name;
> Or, if thou wilt not, be but—"

She broke off in the middle of the line, frankly giggling now at herself. Then she slid down from the window and grew business-like, heat or no heat. She slipped off her dress, mended a runner in her stockings, brushed her hair vigorously for five minutes and then threw herself down in the Grand-Rapids-golden-oak-hall-bedroom rocker, lit a cigarette and relaxed.

She leaned her head against the stiff chair, and sprawled her long, graceful legs in front of her and watched the humid dark slowly settle over the sweltering city. Tomorrow there was a job—of a sort. Something to fill in, to keep her going until . . .

Her mind drifted with the smoke into a realm of daydreams that were the essence of unfulfilled reality.

She couldn't have told exactly when she first noticed the strange odor. It seemed to creep up on her, slowly to pervade the room, alien and somehow ominous. She sat up and sniffed. There *was* a smell. It wasn't just her imagination. She sniffed again. Heavy, pungent, slightly sickish. Gas!

She crossed quickly to the other side of the room, where a screen shielded the table that held a single gas ring. But it wasn't as strong there as it was near the door into the hall. She lit a match, guided it along the connecting coils, but there was no sudden spurt of flame.

She went to the door, opened it and stepped into the hall. But there was no gas connection there. Just a dim, electric bulb, faintly illuminating the pale, peeling walls and the faded carpet. To the right was a narrow stairway leading down.

The odor was stronger here at the head of the stairs. She hesitated a moment, then ran down quickly.

There was another dim, electric bulb and two doors leading into the hall below. One of the doors was open and she could see that the room was empty. She paused before the other one, uncertain. The odor was very strong now. She knocked, waited. There was no answer. She flung the door open quickly.

She staggered back and clapped a hand over mouth and nose against the rush of heavy, sickening air. Her eyes pierced the gloom beyond the doorway and she uttered a startled cry.

The window was closed and the curtain down. The screen before a table, identical with the one in her own room, was pushed aside, and there was a soft, deadly sighing coming from the gas ring. And on the bed, dimly seen in the deepening twilight, was a figure.

For a moment she stood there swaying, sudden panic clutching at her throat. Then she sprang forward toward the window and sent it crashing to the top. She leaped toward the gas ring, swiftly stilled its ominous hissing. One hand darted to the electric light switch and another snatched a towel from the washstand. She beat about her fiercely, pushing the fetid gas toward the window, striving to create a tent of air above the prostrate figure.

She was choking and gasping, but her brain was working quickly. The landlady was out. There were no other tenants in the house. The telephone was in the basement four floors below. It would take her minutes, and in the meantime . . .

Remnants of emergency first aid wisdom flashed through her mind. She straightened twisted limbs, started the steady rhythm of artificial respiration. Arms up . . . above the head . . . down slow . . . press against the ribs . . . firm, hard, press . . . then arms up again . . . over and over, endlessly repeated . . . five minutes . . . ten . . . up, down, press . . .

There was a moan, weak at first, then louder, anguished, as if it were tearing its way upward from some deep well of pain as it burst from the pale lips. Dark, shadowed eyelids fluttered. A hand moved, groping. Eyes opened. Lost eyes, filled with aching torment.

Helen Varney ceased the slow, arm-to-arm rhythm and sank back onto a chair beside the bed. She was breathing heavily and sweat beaded her forehead and upper lip. For the first time she really looked at the girl before her.

Dark hair and eyes, very much like her own. Young, too. Maybe twenty-two or three. And tall, as she was herself. But there the resemblance ceased.

She went to the washstand and soaked a rag with cold water and bathed the girl's face and forehead and neck. Her eyes were closed again now, but she breathed evenly. She lay thus for a long time, and there was no sound in the hot little room. Only the muted noises of the city at night.

At last she spoke in a voice of tragic weariness. "Why—" It was a half whisper, accusing, bitter. "Why didn't you let me—*go?*"

Helen Varney did not answer, for there was no answer. But she put out her hand and gently brushed back the dark hair from the tired white forehead.

There are some moments in life that are the distilled essence of tragedy, moments when the human spirit, shorn of its pitiful defenses, stands naked. And this was one of them.

A girl, desperate, tormented, anguished, had sought death. And another girl had snatched her back to life. In one quick instant a bond was forged. A bond of bitterness and pity. Bitterness toward one who had prevented escape into the lovely nirvana of eternity. Pity for one so desperate and driven that life offered no solace but death.

The girl on the bed rose weakly on one elbow, struggling to sit up.

"Lie quiet. Don't try—"

"No." Her voice was harsh now, and she brushed aside the other's gentle hands. "No." And she pulled herself upright, swaying unsteadily. "Didn't you ever want to—to die?" It was an accusation against one who had robbed her. It was a defense of her own action. "Didn't you?"

"Please! You mustn't—"

"What do you know about it? What do you know about what I must and mustn't?" Her voice grew stronger, took on the shrill edge of hysteria. "Why did you have to come in here and stop me? Why didn't you let me go? Let me escape, let me get out of it—the whole awful, dirty mess? Why couldn't you stay away—why—"

This time the gentle hands took on new firmness, pressed the babbling, hysterical girl back onto the pillows, let the flood of accusation and bitter defiance run its course in the blessed relief of great, searing sobs torn from torment and loneliness. The girl's body trembled and shivered, even in the sultry night, as she clutched the bedclothes, the gentle, ministering hands, her own heavy, disheveled hair.

But presently she grew quieter. The frantic fluttering of her hands was stilled, and the sobs and tears and weeping that racked her brought easement from suffering. When she spoke again it was only in tragic exhaustion. No more accusation or defiance. Only a sort of reaching out toward another, a weary seeking for the solace of human contact.

"Didn't you—" The voice was quiet now. "Didn't you ever want to die?"

"No." Softly. "No, I've always wanted to live."

There was a little silence.

"Haven't you?"

"Yes—in a way."

The girl beside the bed rose and stretched her long arms above her head to ease tired muscles. The fight for that other life had not been easy. Only now that it was over did she begin to feel the effects of the struggle.

She looked down at the other girl and felt a surge of compassion, an urge to help her over the dark span where she had been so perilously poised. The girl herself had given her a lead. Make her forget if only for a little while the thing she had been running away from. Blot out for a brief hour the bitterness of one life in the simple account of another's.

Helen Varney sniffed the air. It was clear now. No heavy sickness of gas. There was a package of cigarettes on the dresser and a folder of matches. She helped herself, offered one to the girl on the bed, but the girl shook her head. Then she flung herself down in the chair again and let her weary body rest.

She blew a long, contemplative cloud of smoke before she spoke. Then she laughed slightly, deprecatingly. "I have, in a way. I mean lived. But it hasn't been very exciting. Up to this time it's all been sort of ordinary and dullish. You see, I . . ."

It was a simple tale, one that had been retold so often, in both fact and fiction, that it had taken on the character of a cliché. The small town girl with ambition—the "bright lights of the Great White Way"—the traveling road show . . .

"There really are a few left," she said, "although the going's getting awfully tough, what with the movies in every tank town along the line. I'd always wanted two things—to be an actress and to get away from Aunt Sophy. My people died when I was about twelve, and she was the only relative I had, and I had to live with her. I didn't hate her. I was just bored to death with righteousness and routine.

"So about two years ago, when I was twenty, I managed to get a job in this road show and I ran away. I've never heard from her since, and I think she has officially disowned me as an abandoned woman. Once I sent her a photograph just for fun. What she'd really like, probably, is one dressed to the ears. Or rather undressed. Looking like Vice and Sin incarnate, so she could show it to all the neighbors and say, 'See, what did I tell you?' So I fooled her. I sent her one all done up for a character part—a nice old lady with glasses and a shawl and gray hair and wrinkles."

She laughed.

"And now," the other girl said, "you're in New York at last, and you're going to be a great actress and live happily ever after." There was weary mockery in her tone, but Helen Varney disregarded it.

"Yes," she said, "I'm here, and I'm going to be an actress. But not right away. For a while, I guess, I'll have to be a waitress."

"Something of a comedown."

"And how! But I've got to eat and pay rent until I get a break. I've been here five weeks and I've tried to see every manager in town. I owe three weeks' rent, so tomorrow I go to work as a wait-ress in one of the Jason restaurants. I've got just fifty cents left."

She threw her head back and sent three perfect smoke rings into the still air.

The face of the girl on the bed twisted with an ironic smile. "You've only got fifty cents to your name and you're full of life. I've got fifty th—" She broke off in sudden confusion, then added hastily as if to cover her own discomposure, "You don't seem downhearted."

"Oh, I'm not. I'll get a break sometime. Then I'll be all set. I'm not discouraged. But I do get *mad*. At managers! If I could only get in to see them I know I could put myself over. I'm a pretty good actress. I'm going to be a lot better. Someday maybe I'll be a headliner. All I need is a chance. I know that. If I could only get at one of 'em. Just one. A man like John Golden or Gilbert Miller or Hugo Steinmark. There's a man I'd like to work for. He's doing new things in the theater. He doesn't go along in the same old rut. He—"

She paused abruptly, looked at the girl on the bed. "My dear, what is it? What—"

"Oh, nothing, nothing. I just— Please go on. You want to work for Hugo Steinmark, but you can't get an interview. You're going to be a great actress. Go on! Go on!" The voice had grown harsh again.

"But there's not anything more to tell."

"There's nothing more to tell because you can't get an interview with Hugo Steinmark; so you're going to be a waitress, but some-day— Oh, that's funny! You don't know how funny it is. That—" She was laughing now. Not a laughing laugh, but one filled with mock-ery and edged again with hysteria. "Here, give me that bag—there on the dresser. I'll show you how funny it is. I'll show— There, read that."

She dug into an expensive seal leather handbag and brought out an envelope. She ripped a note from it and held it out. "Read that. Read it and then you'll know why I'm laughing."

The girl beside the bed read it. It was very short, written on heavy white note paper, and at the top there was an address. Num-ber 3 Evergreen Drive. "Dear Miss Starr: I will see you Thursday evening about nine o'clock at my home at the above address. You need not give your name to the maid when you call. Simply say you have an appointment with me. Hugo Steinmark."

Helen Varney's eyes went wide as she read the magic signature. Hugo Steinmark! Strange, meteoric genius of the theater and finance. Risen in ten years from a penniless alien to the dizzy pinnacle of the multifarious Steinmark enterprises. Theatrical real estate. Producing companies. Lush musicals. The superintellectual experimental drama. Holding contracts of a dozen of the most glamorous names of the American theater.

Hugo Steinmark! A name to conjure with. Helen Varney looked at the other girl enviously, incredulously.

"You've got a date with Hugo Steinmark for day after tomorrow and you're trying to commit suicide. That doesn't make sense."

"Maybe not to you."

"Are you an actress? Are you on the stage here? Are you . . ." She poured out an eager flood of questions, but the other shook her head wearily.

"No, no. I'm not an actress. I'm just a—" She threw herself back onto the pillows again and closed her eyes. "I can't tell you what I am. I don't know myself. It's all so—so complicated." She laughed a little and it was shot through with irony.

"I've had too much excitement and you haven't had enough. You're trying to be an actress and I'm trying to be a corpse. I'm committing suicide because I have a date day after tomorrow with Hugo Steinmark. And you'd give your eyeteeth to be in my place. I've got—"

She broke off suddenly. She didn't say anything for a minute. Then she rose slowly on her elbow again. She looked the other girl up and down, from the heavy dark hair to the long, graceful legs.

"And you'd give your eyeteeth to be in my place." She repeated her own statement softly, addressing herself rather than the other girl. She frowned a little with a thought that seemed hovering behind her troubled eyes.

"Get up," she said. "Now turn around slowly." She nodded her head approvingly as the other girl obeyed. "What's your name?"

"Helen Varney."

"That's nice and simple. Try that—there in the closet—that jacket. . . . Now hold the skirt against you, too. . . . We're almost the same size, aren't we?"

"Yes. Yes, we are." It was a little puzzling.

She laid the suit—the label was Bergdorf, Goodman—over the end of the bed and sat down once more. The other girl was still eying her, appraising her. The frown flickered into a hesitant smile.

"How—how would you like to live at the Waldorf-Astoria instead of a hall bedroom?"

"Who wouldn't?"

"Then listen." The other girl was suddenly eager. "You say your life's been dull. That nothing very exciting or thrilling has ever happened to you. Well, here's your chance. What do you say?"

"What do I say to what?"

"My name is—" She hesitated a moment. Then came out with it. "Joanna Starr. Yours is Helen Varney. We exchange names—and all that goes with them. Do you understand? You get everything you want. Excitement, thrills—danger maybe. And I get everything I want. Escape into something simple and dull. Waiting on table. Serving people food. Plain and uncomplicated and useful."

Helen Varney laughed indulgently. "But people don't go around exchanging names and being someone they're not. What would your people say? Your friends, relatives?"

"I haven't got any people or friends or rela—" She broke off and bitterness took possession of her again. "I haven't got *anybody*. Do you understand that, anybody? No one cares whether I live or die. Whether I'm here or not here."

Helen Varney's voice softened. "Is that why you were trying to . . ." She left the sentence unfinished, but she gestured significantly in the direction of the gas jet.

The other girl didn't answer. Caution seemed to mix itself with the bitterness, as if she repelled even this gentle probing. Caution—and then fear.

It showed in her eyes, in the instinctive contraction of her shoulders, in the sudden stillness of her whole body, as if her veins were slowly invaded by ice and her muscles stiffened with alarm. It was a hunted, haunted look of someone running away, and Helen Varney, watching, cursed herself for her own ineptness.

She put out her hands impulsively and grasped the other girl's cold ones as if to transmit some of her own warmth and courage.

"Don't. Don't think about it, whatever it was."

"That's what I'm trying to do." She paused. Fear receded slightly and the little thought hovered again behind her troubled eyes. She braced herself, and her voice grew steadier. And calculating.

"Funny, what you said. 'People don't go around being someone they're not.' Actresses do."

"On the stage. Not in real life."

"But you haven't been able to get on the stage. Not the real stage. Not Broadway. You've tramped the pavements for five weeks trying to see managers. You haven't much chance against that closed corporation. No pull, no influence; you don't know anybody. It must be dreary to think of being a waitress or a clerk in a store or a bundle wrapper all your life."

"Oh, but I won't. I'm an actress and a pretty good one. I've got to have a chance though."

"That's it. You've got to have a chance to show your stuff. Don't you see? That's what I'm offering you. A chance to see Hugo Steinmark. This"—and she indicated the note on the heavy white paper "—this is part of the bargain, you know."

Helen Varney didn't say anything for a moment. Then, "If you're not an actress, what were you going to see Hugo Steinmark about?"

Joanna Starr shook her head decisively. "No. You take it as is—or leave it. I'm giving you the chance to see him. That's what you want, isn't it? Well, here it is—on a silver platter."

"But I—"

Joanna Starr seized upon the hesitation.

"You mean you're not a good gambler? You never play poker for money? Just matches? Is that what you mean? Look, my dear, I know a little about stage people myself. And they're all gamblers. The good ones. They'll risk everything they've got on a thousand-to-one chance. That's the way most of 'em win out. You talk about getting a break. You don't get a break. You seize onto it. And if you don't seize onto it, it's gone forever and you're still a road show actress or a waitress."

The note from Hugo Steinmark was in her hand. She tapped it slowly, tantalizingly. She leaned forward again and laid her hand over Helen Varney's, a new excited urgency in her tone.

"Call it a dare, if you want to. Or a new thrilling adventure. A challenge. Call it your first big role. The scenes are already sketched in, and they're full of all the things you've missed so far. But you haven't any lines yet. You'll have to make them up as you go along. And the stage is all set. There's a room at the Waldorf in the name of Joanna Starr. There's a closet full of beautiful clothes. And there's—"

She broke off, waited.

"And there's the chance to see Hugo Steinmark?"

She nodded. "The chance to see Hugo Steinmark."

It was true, what the other had said about seizing onto a break. About the gamble. About the thousand-to-one chance. It was all true. And it was crazy, mad, preposterous.

She thought of the long succession of grimy small town hotels and the drabness of hall bedrooms, of the miles of pavement pounding and the weary waiting in managers' offices. She thought of Hugo Steinmark. A chance to see Hugo Steinmark! Her great chance! Her break!

But most of all she thought of Joanna Starr, of the hunted, haunted look in her eyes, of the pain and bitterness and weariness of her voice when she had found that death had been denied her.

She, Helen Varney, had snatched another life back from death. In some queer way in which destiny and duty were all mixed up, she was responsible for that other life. And in some queer way Joanna Starr clung desperately to the thought of escaping into the dull, safe haven of Helen Varney's name.

Escaping and leaving someone else to play out the scene—*a thrilling, new adventure. if challenge. Your first big role. . . .*

Helen Varney was breathing quickly, uncertainly, but there was excitement in her eyes. For one more moment she hesitated. Then her hands shot out impulsively to meet Joanna Starr's.

2

Joanna Starr lay in the wide, soft bed and purred like a comfortable kitten.

The radium-dialed clock on the bedside table said just nine o'clock. The morning sun came in through the half-drawn shades, and beyond the wide windows she could see it shining on the East River, turning the sullen, dark channel into a broad ribbon of gay, glinting sunlight.

For a while she just lay and let it soak in—the softness of the bed, the freshness of the morning, the room with its rose carpet and gray and gold walls and heavy silken draperies; the silver and crystal of the dressing table, the wadded satin dressing gown flung carelessly over a rose and gold chair.

She sighed deeply from the depth of a hedonist's voluptuous soul and tried to decide whether it would be more pleasurable to leap quickly from the bed and shout and sing, or just lie and continue to purr. The decision was too difficult for a spirit drugged and enfeebled by almost twelve hours of blatant luxury. Instead she reached out a hand and picked up the telephone.

"Room service, please." Just like that. No questions asked. No explanations. Just "Room service," and order anything you want. Strawberries, coffee, toasted muffins. She tried to think of something exotic and thrilling, but breakfast wasn't that kind of meal. She'd make up for it at lunch.

While she waited for the tray, she lay and reviewed the incredible kaleidoscope of events that had brought her, Helen Va— No, no, she wasn't Helen Varney any more. She'd sold that name. Sold it down the river, maybe, but sold it nevertheless. For a chance to see Hugo Steinmark.

She was Joanna Starr. She must remember that. She wondered if the clerks at the desk, the boys in the elevator, the maids and attendants and managers had looked at her queerly when she had come in last night.

In the constant flux of thousands of guests in a great hotel could individual faces register on their crowded memories? Had they any inkling that the Joanna Starr who had left that morning was not the same Joanna Starr who had returned that night? Even though she wore the same clothes, the same smart gray suit with the green linen blouse, the same delightfully outrageous hat? Even though they were roughly the same height, weight, coloring? Same age and same general contour of features?

But no one, of course, who really knew either of them would confuse them. Which made the whole thing all the more ridiculous. It was fantastic, grotesque, melodramatic, improbable, absurd, preposterous! But it was true.

This time yesterday she had been tramping hot pavements with fifty cents in her pocketbook searching for a job. Now she was lying on a bed of roses. She snuggled into the soft pillows with sensual pleasure. Now she was living on milk and honey. "Strawberries, coffee and muffins, coming up!" Or didn't they speak the same language at the Waldorf-Astoria as they did at drugstore lunch counters? Probably not. Now she was clothed in purple and fine linen. She looked toward the open closet door. Sports wear, lingerie, a silver fox scarf.

And tomorrow night she had a date with Hugo Steinmark . . .

And for all this she had traded only a name, a waitress' job in a chain restaurant, and two road-stained suitcases containing a dwindling wardrobe. That and her solemn word of honor that she'd stand by the name of Joanna Starr until . . .

There had been no limit placed on that "until." Nor could questions, however adroit, draw forth anything that was not already encompassed by the tawdry little rooming house room and the tragedy that it had almost witnessed. She recalled the other girl's words:

"We exchange from the soul and skin out. All or nothing. Take it *as is*—or leave it."

And she had taken it. She had signed a blank check for a pig in a poke. Again it was preposterous! She was pledged to stand by the name of Joanna Starr, but she hadn't the slightest idea who Joanna Starr was. Ridiculous! Fantastic!

Of course she could always in an extremity find Joa— find Helen Varney at Unit 7 of Jason Restaurants. But even as she reassured herself, she was ashamed. Figuring out already how she could welsh on her bargain. Muffing her role, even before the curtain was properly up. A fine gambler!

Yes, she repeated, she could always put her hands on Helen Varney. But would she? After all, she had made a bargain.

Only two things that other girl had told her. The first was why she had come to the dreary rooming house.

"The stuff you take is so messy and painful and hard to get, so I got on a streetcar going over Brooklyn Bridge. But I got frightened. The water was so far below and it was so black and dirty. When I got off at the Brooklyn end I just wandered around and then I saw a sign where it said *Housekeeping Room Vacant* and I thought of gas."

The second was a specific admonition.

"There's a suitcase in the clothes closet at the hotel. Heavy brown leather. You'll recognize it because all the other luggage is light gray airplane fabric. Take care of it—I mean the heavy brown one. You may need it someday. Need it badly." And there had been a strange look in her eyes when she had said it.

The bell rang softly. She sprang from bed and wrapped the satin dressing gown around her and went to the door to receive the breakfast tray from a waiter. Then she settled herself comfortably in the easy chair by the window with the tray across the arms.

She yawned luxuriously, and nibbled the fresh berries lying red and luscious against their background of cool green leaves with a flanking mountain of white powdered sugar. She drank the steaming coffee, and buttered three toasted blueberry muffins.

As she stretched like a cat full of cream, her eye fell on a yellow envelope lying on the table. The telegram from Hollywood that had been waiting for her when she had come to the hotel last night. She opened it and reread it.

DARLING YOUR WIRE DELAYED JUST GOT IT YESTERDAY ARRIVE NEW YORK WEDNESDAY VIA PLANE PAUL.

Wednesday. That was today. She was the "darling" of someone named Paul, and he was arriving today, and she wondered who he was. She wondered just how she would explain things to Paul and just how Paul would take her explanation.

That brought up the whole problem of Joanna Starr's friends. Of course the real Joanna had said so vehemently and so bitterly that she had none. But that couldn't be entirely true. A person couldn't live in a vacuum. There must be people, someone, and was she to—

The telephone broke in as if to say, "Make up your mind quickly, because here's one of them now." She felt herself getting flustered and she hesitated slightly before answering. She couldn't think what to say. But that was the trouble. Don't think. Don't plan. Just rely on impulse, on the spur-of-the-moment inspiration.

She picked up the receiver and said "Hello."

"Joanna?" It was a man's voice.

"Yes."

"You weren't trying to run away from me, were you?"

"No—no, I wasn't running away." (The other Joanna had been running away from something, though.)

There was a pause. Then cautiously from the other end of the wire "Is this Joanna?"

"Of course. Who did you think it was? (That was it. Be bold.) Who are *you*, incidentally?"

Another pause.

"Don't you know?"

"No. You sound like—" But he sounded like any one of a hundred masculine voices robbed of individuality by the impersonalizing mechanism of wires and cables. She groped for a line and fumbled. "I mean your voice doesn't seem—"

"Neither does yours."

There was a little click at the other end of the wire. He had hung up.

She laid the receiver back into its cradle thoughtfully. Then she shrugged her shoulders. Round one to the unknown opposition. A gentleman friend of the real Joanna had called up and he hadn't believed her. She wondered again what Paul would say.

Oh, well . . .

She yawned and stretched again and considered what she would wear tomorrow night when she went to see Hugo Steinmark. She slid the hangers along the racks in the closet and surveyed "her" wardrobe. Then a calculating look came into her eyes. A new dress! A really new one. She'd worn seconds for such a long time. Shopping! It would be exciting.

She crossed to the dresser and snatched the heavy seal leather handbag from the top drawer. There was a wad of bills in it, a big wad. Might be a good idea to count it and see how long she could continue to support Joanna Starr in the manner to which she was obviously accustomed.

That other Joanna had been very insistent about the money. She had taken the fifty cent piece and given a wad of bills as big as your fist in exchange, and protest only brought forth the inevitable, "All or nothing. You take this [indicating the bills] and spend it as you please [curious emphasis there], or you don't take anything. And that includes the chance to see Hugo Steinmark."

That, of course, had clinched it.

The new Joanna snapped the rubber band off the roll of bills and flipped it open. She blinked. There was a five hundred dollar bill on top. She'd never seen one before and she examined it curiously.

"Five hundred dollars." She repeated the sum aloud. She blinked again as she picked it up and saw that the bill underneath was also for five hundred dollars. She turned the roll over. The bill on the bottom was of the same denomination.

Her brows knit in a puzzled frown. She hesitated. Then quickly she leafed through the roll, counting . . . three, four . . . sixty-two . . . seventy-nine . . . ninety-nine, one hundred! And they were all five hundred dollar bills! One hundred five hundred dollar bills! *Fifty thousand dollars!*

She had fifty thousand dollars there in one fist! She had given that other girl her sole remaining fifty cent piece, and she'd gotten fifty thousand dollars in return! She suddenly felt her hands trembling.

There flashed through her mind a phrase. *Poker for money.*

This was money! She remembered the phrase and the queer smile of that other girl, the strange expression on her face as she had made the exchange. The exchange of a fifty cent piece in a worn pocketbook for an expensive seal leather handbag containing fifty thousand dollars!

3

But there had been that curious emphasis when the other girl had said, "Spend it as you please." So she did.

Not all of it, of course. And not without scruples. But a new dress anyway. *The* new dress for the meeting tomorrow night with Hugo Steinmark. With all the fixings.

Never before had she shopped without the constraint of a budget. Now in the shops to which the wad of bills was an open sesame, the mere mention of price seemed a vulgarity.

There was, first of all, the dress. Pale lilac trimmed with fuchsia, and a large, soft handkerchief of fuchsia chiffon splashed with purple pansies. There was an evening jacket of fuchsia velvet, lilac slippers with delicately jeweled heels, a lilac evening bag to match.

"And I'll send myself an orchid," she promised, and laughed.

It all took time and it was late when she got back to the hotel. She was hot and tired and wanted nothing so much as a cool shower. Hardly the mood for mystery. And yet that's what she found. Not a big mystery. Just an ordinary, medium-sized one to add to those which were slowly accumulating about her life as Joanna Starr.

When she called at the desk for her key, the clerk who handed it to her detached a memorandum. "A gentleman to, see you," he said. "He called about an hour ago and said that he would wait in the lobby. He asked to be paged when you came in. A Mr. Hutton."

Joanna tried to look as if she and Mr. Hutton were old friends. "All right, page Mr. Hutton."

"If you'll just step into the lobby . . ."

The bellboy was persistent and thorough. "Calling Mr. Hutton . . . Mr. Hutton . . ." And Joanna herself stood at the entrance to the lobby and surveyed the sprinkling of men and speculated on which one Mr. Hutton might be and what she would say to him. But Mr. Hutton was not there apparently, and finally both Joanna and the bellboy gave up.

As she rode up in the elevator she wondered if Mr. Hutton might by any chance have been the skeptical gentleman who had telephoned that morning. Skeptical, and he'd come to check up, to see for himself. If he had been in the lobby he could easily have seen her. Seen her and known that she was not really Joanna Starr. In that case . . .

She tried to recall what the men in the lobby looked like, but most of them had been hidden behind newspapers. There had been one tall, blond one like a moving picture Apollo, and one medium-sized, dark one who was so-so, and a redheaded college boy—at least he looked like a college boy—and an elderly gentleman with a white goatee like a Southern colonel. There were others, too. But she couldn't remember them all.

Oh, well . . .

Her purchases had preceded her by special messenger, and she tore into the pile of shining bristol boxes like a child on Christmas morning, lifting the lilac gown from its tissue wrapping, laying it out tenderly upon the bed.

She sang under the shower, and dried off with lovely, deep-napped, half-acre towels. She dusted her skin with fragrant bath powder, and slipped into a dressing gown of daffodil silk embroidered in misty pastels of blue and mauve and faint greens like the first pale shoots of spring in the garden.

With a sigh of great bodily content she stretched out in grateful weariness on the chaise longue, lit a cigarette and gazed idly through the evening paper she had brought with her from her shopping expedition. Silly, buying a paper. The want ads didn't mean anything to her now. She laughed at her own instinctive reaction. She could, of course, as a last resort read the news.

A politician had made a speech. A ball player had made two homers, and his picture was on the front page right beside that of a visiting celebrity.

". . . Trudi Hess, Austrian actress and Hollywood star, scheduled to make two pictures in the East, who arrived this morning via special plane accompanied by . . ."

She folded the paper and settled more comfortably to a review of the retinue of Trudi Hess. There was an actress for you! Not that Joanna admired her acting so much, but she liked her offstage technique. Glamour on a grand scale. Extravagance of personality, the kind the public demands in its play actors. Trudi Hess had it.

". . . accompanied by her father, Otto Hess, two maids, a secretary, fifteen trunks and a half-tame cheetah."

The telephone rang. Joanna flung down the paper and reached for the receiver. Perhaps it was Mr. Hutton, whoever he was.

"Hello." Cool and unconcerned.

"Darling! Darling, is it really you?"

It was a man's voice, a voice that was deep and rich and seemed to project itself into the room even through the mechanical barrier of the telephone.

It was Paul. It must be. And she was his "darling." Darling wife, mistress or fiancée? She felt some strange emotion teasing the ends of her nerves.

When she had first received the wire she had put off thinking of Paul and the complications his arrival would bring. He wasn't important. Nothing in her fantastic new life was important but the date with Hugo Steinmark. Somehow, she had told herself, when situations arose she would handle them. But she wouldn't worry about them beforehand.

She hadn't worried about Paul and his coming. And now here he was on the other end of the line. And suddenly he, too, seemed important. Not to her, of course. But to that other Joanna.

Even while she stood there hesitating with the receiver at her ear, a flash of understanding illuminated the mystery behind that pitiful attempt at suicide in the dark little room of the Brooklyn brownstone.

YOUR WIRE DELAYED JUST GOT IT YESTERDAY ARRIVE . . .

Suddenly she knew what she must do, promises or no promises to that other Joanna. But she couldn't do it over the telephone.

"Jo!" The voice cut in, peremptory, puzzled by her silence. "Jo, is it you? Are you there?"

"Yes, yes, of course. And you're Paul, aren't you?"

"Of course." Still puzzled. Then he laughed. It was a nice laugh. She liked it. "Or do lots of other men call you 'darling'?"

"Only on Tuesday and Thursday of alternate weeks. Listen, I must see you."

"You must see—" He sounded nonplused. "Well, my dear, I rather thought that was the idea. I mean that's why I flew over three thousand miles, wasn't it? So you could see me?"

"Yes, of course." How stupid of her! "And the sooner the better. Suppose—" Her eye had fallen on the lilac evening gown spread across the bed. "Where are you now?"

"I've just gotten myself and my luggage settled at the Wessex. The Waldorf's much too grand for me."

"Suppose you unpack your white tie and tails and take me to dinner tonight. Call for me about seven."

There was a little silence. Then, "Jo, darling, is it— Your voice doesn't sound natural."

"I know. But it's the telephone. No one ever sounds natural over the telephone."

"Yes, of course. But you seem—gay and excited."

"I am gay and excited. I have a gorgeous new dress, and a handsome gentleman is taking me out to dinner. Or is he?"

"Why, yes. Yes, of course." But there was a puzzled restraint in his voice. "I'll be there at seven." And he hung up.

She put the receiver back in its cradle and smiled. It all seemed so plain now. What it was all about and what she must do about it.

Joanna Starr, the real Joanna, had been in love and in trouble. Either one was bad enough, but the combination had proved almost fatal. She had wired the man she had been in love with to help her out of the trouble. And he had let her down.

Or that's what she had thought. And so she had tried to die. But he hadn't really let her down. YOUR WIRE DELAYED JUST GOT IT YESTERDAY. And he had come three thousand miles through the air as fast as a plane could bring him. Just one of those petty, silly misunderstandings against which two lives had almost come to tragedy. Well, perhaps she could do something about *that*.

When the telephone rang almost on the dot of seven o'clock she was just slipping her toes into the jeweled slippers.

"Mr. Paul Saniel to see Miss Starr."

"Tell him I'll be right— No, ask him to come up, please."

"Yes, Miss Starr."

Saniel. Paul Saniel. That was a nice name. Silly, that first idea of meeting him downstairs. How would she know him and he her? She laughed a little in anticipation of his bewilderment when she opened the door and he would be faced with a completely strange woman.

But quite a nice-looking one really. She surveyed herself in the long glass approvingly and gave the fuchsia handkerchief with the splatter of purple pansies that hung from a crystal bracelet on her left arm a graceful, lighthearted swish through the air.

She could play a part in a gown like this. A society glamour girl, a toothpaste and cigarette ad come-on, a woman of mystery. She looked alternately gay, grinning and enigmatic.

She wondered if Paul had a sense of humor. She hoped so. He'd need it and a lot more when she first opened the door and evaded the inevitable rush of arms anxious to encompass his "darling." She wondered again whether she was supposed to be his darling wife, fiancée or mistress.

The bell rang.

Joanna Starr took one last approving glance at herself in the long mirror and crossed the room to open the door.

4

She opened the door—and stepped back.

But the man standing there made no passionate rush to encompass her in his arms. He just stood there. And looked at her. And she looked at him.

Tall. Broad shoulders, too, that filled out the dinner jacket with a hint of strength and power. Black hair springing crisply from a wide forehead. in the early thirties, perhaps. The mouth was full and sensitive. But unsmiling. The eyes . . .

She felt herself caught up and held by the deep-set, dark eyes. For there was no expression in them. None at all. Not after that first quick, penetrating glance when she had opened the door. It was as if he were blind. But he wasn't. He was looking at her. She could feel it. She could feel him looking at her and beyond her and around her and through her. Taking in everything. Her, the room, the dressing gown over the foot of the bed.

But she couldn't see him. She couldn't see into him. She couldn't get past those expressionless eyes. His face was like a house with blank shades pulled down and someone hiding and peeping from behind them.

Slowly the gaiety and laughter seemed to grow cold within her, to congeal. She felt a shiver run through her nerves. She thought suddenly of that other Joanna, and this man before her, and knew that her conclusions had been too facile. And she had intended bringing two sundered hearts together, erasing tragedy.

"Hello, Jo," he said, and walked into the room.

"Oh, hello—Paul." She tried to match the coolness and casualness of his voice, as she took up the challenge of his two simple words.

Hello, Jo. No surprise. No astonishment. No bewildering questions. And all the time he knew, he must know, that in place of his "darling" there was an impostor. Sleeping in her room, using her name, wearing her clothes, dining with her—

She couldn't fill in the blank. She didn't know what this man was to the real Joanna Starr. She only knew that he was playing a part, one that he had seized upon in the fraction of a second following that first swift glance when she had opened the door.

He was playing a part, wary, cautious, calculating. She must play one, too. Take her cues from him, but match him play for play.

"Paul, my dear," she said in her best English-drawing-room-comedy-drama voice, as she reached for the velvet jacket and her evening bag, "shall we start off with a cocktail in the Cert Room?"

"Yes, let's do. Here, let me help you," as he held her jacket for her. "Ghastly weather in the plane. I'll enjoy a steady meal again."

She laughed—oh, so casually and full of lighthearted irony. "And I'm just in the mood for dinner in one of those places on the ninety-ninth floor or the roof, that makes you feel as if you were up in an airplane."

But he was a gentleman true to the traditions of English-drawing-room comedy drama, so they compromised on the Rainbow Room.

They floated on top of Manhattan as if they were in some unreal and yet tangible ship, at anchor above a dark, amorphous mass that was the city. A city that might at any moment suck them down into its unknown depths.

Or was it their conversation that lent color to such fantasy? It sailed along lightly, skimming the innocuous surface, filled with trivia, inconsequential, unrevealing.

And yet at any moment in danger of sinking into a morass of truth, of accusation and questions and demands.

"Shall we dance?"

"Yes, the music's marvelous."

They danced. As if they had danced together all their lives. Eyes followed them. So well matched, so tall, so graceful. A handsome man and a beautiful woman. And the fuchsia handkerchief at her wrist floated softly on the air.

"Look, you can almost see Yonkers."

"Not Yonkers. White Plains."

"No, White Plains is over that way, Yonkers is . . ."

She tried to imagine the real Joanna Starr in her place, sitting opposite this man who had flown the continent at her command. What would they be doing? What would they be saying? When she thought he was engaged with the menu she looked at him covertly—and found that he was using it only as a shield to look at her. Their eyes met for a brief moment. Then dropped.

"Coffee?"

"No, it's too hot."

"Perhaps a liqueur?"

"Yes, please. Benedictine."

"Waiter, two benedictines."

It was fantastic and unreal. He knew she was not Joanna Starr. And she knew that he knew it. And he knew that she knew that he knew it. And she knew . . . You could go on endlessly, like a mirror reflecting a reflection that in turn was reflecting, until vertigo sent your brain spinning.

She wondered how long it would go on. How long both of them could keep it up. The empty clichés were beginning to play on her taut nerves like a rasp.

Something must happen. A fire. A waiter breaking dishes with an awful crash. Anything. She hazarded another covert glance at him. His jaw seemed tighter and the baffling blankness of his eyes was slowly giving way to the look of one carefully maneuvering for position.

It was coming now. She wasn't quite sure what "it" was, and in the uncertainty of suspense she felt dizziness creeping upon her. She gave herself a resolute mental shake. No time for nonsense now.

When it did come it was quiet. But a passionate quietness, like a muffler around steel.

"Where is she?"

Just that. Just three brief words. Where is she? Where was Joanna Starr? The real Joanna. The weeping, fear-racked girl of the gas-filled room. The girl who had been running away. From *him?*

She felt all her nerves quivering and she clenched her hands in her lap so that he wouldn't see the whitening knuckles. She felt again that surge of compassion for the defeated, tormented girl in the dark rooming house. The girl whose life was in part hers, because she had snatched it from death. What she had saved she must shield.

"Where is she?" He repeated the question with rising emotion.

She lifted her chin and threw back her head and looked at him directly. "Where you can't find her."

"What have you done to her? Answer me. Where is she?"

His hand shot out and grabbed her wrist and she felt his fingers digging into her flesh, felt pent-up emotion bursting from him, felt his eyes boring into her as if he would tear the answer from her.

He leaned across the table. She drew back.

"*Where is—*"

"The liqueurs, sir." The waiter, quiet, obsequious, impervious and unseeing.

The steel band upon her wrist loosened. She could see his hand trembling as it withdrew. She could see his jaw working and his breath coming quickly.

The waiter set down the two liqueur glasses and left. Now it was her turn.

"Who are you? What are you to Joanna Starr?" Her voice was as cold and hard as his.

"Who are you to ask? An impostor. I can turn you over to the police."

She didn't reply immediately. She just sat there, taut, alert, knowing it was true. It was true—but one line from her could stop him. *Unit 7, Jason Restaurants.* Tell him that. That would stop him. And betray the real Joanna. Betray her, perhaps, to the very thing that had driven her to the awful despair of death. And betray her own honor and pride.

"Do you understand? I can turn you over to the police."

He could, and he would, unless— She summoned all her courage and wily skill. Maybe he was only bluffing. Well, you could fight bluff with bluff.

"You can, of course," she admitted cautiously, "but I wouldn't if I were you."

"No?"

"No. I might be even less willing to talk to the police than to you."

"There are ways of making a person talk."

"I know. But I'm not the person. So you see, if you really want to find out where she is, I wouldn't advise you to be—ah—shall we say precipitate."

She could see him pause, hesitate. It was working.

She had an ace up her sleeve after all.

"What do you want? Money?" he demanded.

"I've got plenty of that."

"Then what's your game?"

"Suppose you answer my question. What are you to Joanna Starr?"

"I'm—" He started to speak, broke off, and a new hardness set his jaw. "No, no. I don't lay down my cards until you've called me."

"I'm calling you right now. What are you to her?"

"Put in your ante. Where is she?"

Impasse! The passionately irresistible force. The stubborn, unmoving, impenetrable object. Head on, smashing into each other.

And all around them people laughed and chatted and ate and danced and the soft night breeze stirred the fuchsia handkerchief with the purple pansies.

A clock high on a tower outlined against the black sky of the night marked nine o'clock, and its deep booming floated on the air above the noise of the city and the music of the dance floor.

Nine o'clock!

Even while they fenced and parried, circled and maneuvered, and his vehemence and urgency and anger battered itself against the stubbornness of her resolve to silence—even while all this was going on, the booming of the clock flashed a thought through her brain.

This time tomorrow night she would be seeing Hugo Steinmark!

The clock struck and struck again. Ten o'clock. Eleven. It made the full circle to nine in the morning. Thursday morning. And from its high tower it looked down on the city moiling below and went on its course until it had completed another full circle.

It was nine o'clock on Thursday evening . . . and then ten . . . ten-thirty . . . The clock pealed the half-hour.

Its deep clang was muted by the heavy silken draperies of the room in rose and gray and gold as the girl who had taken the name of Joanna Starr tried to locate the lock of the door with hands that were icy and shaking.

The key caught and she managed to twist it in spite of the trembling of her hands. The door swung open and she almost fell into the room. She closed it quickly behind her and stood leaning against it, fighting the nervous tremor that was creeping through her whole body.

She staggered across the room and groped for the bed. She didn't turn on the light. She didn't want light. She wanted darkness like a protective blanket, like a deep cave where one might hide and be safe from the horror that pursued.

She reached for the wadded dressing gown and pulled it around her shoulders. Far below the city sweltered. But she was cold. Her limbs jerked convulsively and she grabbed hold of the footboard to steady herself. She kicked off the lilac slippers with the jeweled heels and drew her feet up under her and huddled there at the foot of the bed, trembling, trying to blot out horror and fear and the panic of flight.

And the moonlight coming in through the east window caught the shine of the jeweled heels and set them twinkling gaily. But because it was moonlight and unreal, it veiled the reality of wet grass tarnish and tiny daubs of dried mud that still clung to the soles.

And, spread across the right toe, the heavy, brown stain . . .

5

Inspector Frye of the Homicide Squad looked at the clock which stood on the desk of the small anteroom which he had commandeered for his use in the Steinmark house. It was just half an hour after midnight.

At his right a detective sat with notebook and pencil. At his left was a tall, handsome, blond fellow. His name, as the detective had taken it down in his notebook, was Theron O'Hara.

"I tell you, I don't know," O'Hara was saying. "I was upstairs most of the time."

"But you were in the house?"

"Of course. I'm not denying that."

"O. K. then. Start from the beginning."

"Well, I was here for dinner."

"Invited or did you just drop in?"

"Invited. Steinmark called me early in the morning and said he wanted me to come out for dinner and stay the night."

"Any indication what he wanted you for?"

"Nothing definite. Just a hint. 'Stay all night. I'll need you in the morning—maybe.' Like that, with a short hesitation before the 'maybe.'"

"How long have you known him?"

"Only about ten days."

"Then you're not his regular legal adviser?"

"No. The firm of Howland and Storm handles all the legal business of the Steinmark enterprises."

"Then why was he consulting you?"

"He said it was a personal matter that had no connection with the theatrical producing enterprise. When he first came to see me ten days ago, the call was, you might say, in the nature of a feeler. He asked me if I would be willing to act for him in a delicate personal matter."

"But that's it. What was it? The delicate personal matter?"

"He didn't tell me. I said that I would have to know more about it before I made a decision. I was a bit curious and asked him why he had selected me. He said that he had investigated me carefully and that I had the kind of practice that fitted me to deal with this particular matter."

"And what kind of a practice have you?"

"Mostly pretty confidential work. Divorce cases, blackmail, scandal suits. Out of court, you understand. That's my business. Keeping 'em out of court."

"I see. But Steinmark gave no indication of the nature of his business?"

"No. Not when he first came to see me. I rather think, though, that he intended to discuss the matter with me last night."

"And did he?"

"No."

"But you talked with him all during dinner and afterward. What did you talk about?"

"Oh, this and that. Nothing of particular consequence. We discovered we both played golf at the same Long Island club. Things like that. And he seemed interested in the Newberger case and we discussed that for quite a while. You remember the Newberger kidnaping last year. I once handled some business for Newberger years ago before he made all his money."

"Anything else you discussed?"

"Nothing that seems to stick in my mind."

"All right. Go on. You came out to dinner. And then what?"

"We had dinner and then coffee and cigars in the drawing room."

"How did he seem? Depressed, excited, moody, uneasy, or what?"

"No, as a matter of fact he seemed to be in a particular good humor. As if—as if he were secretly rather pleased about something."

"You two were alone?"

"Yes. Soon after dinner most of the servants went out. Their night off, I believe. That left only the housekeeper, Mrs. Jacobson. While we were sitting there smoking, she announced a visitor. A Mr. Conway or Connery or something of the sort. I didn't pay much attention.

"She said he was waiting in the library down at the end of the hall. I was left alone, so I finished the cigar I was smoking and then went upstairs to the room which had been assigned to me. It was a little after eight. I read for a while, and when I heard the shot I—"

"Just a minute. Not so fast. You say you went upstairs a little after eight. How long was it before you heard the shot?"

"An hour or more. It was nine-twenty-five exactly when the shot was fired."

"How do you know so 'exactly'?"

"The first thing I did was to look at my watch. You'll probably regard that as highly suspicious, won't you? But remember that I'm a lawyer, and under the circumstances I would be more likely to think of things like that than the ordinary person."

"Was there anything which happened between the time you went upstairs and nine-twenty-five that you consider significant?"

"Possibly. Mrs. Jacobson, though, can tell you better than I. Once during that time I heard a woman's voice."

"Mrs. Jacobson's?"

"No, no. I mean another woman's voice. It sounded as if it might be a much younger woman. It was hot and I left my door open and I heard Mrs. Jacobson talking to a woman down in the hall. Low at first, and then there must have been some kind of rumpus. The other woman's voice got rather loud."

"Could you hear what they were saying?"

"No. Except one scrap of a sentence. It was something about, 'I'll see him if I have to break—' And then I didn't get the rest. And presently the rumpus, or the argument or whatever it was died down and I didn't hear anything more until the sound of the shot.

I had undressed by that time, but I hadn't brought any dressing gown with me. I tried to locate one in one of the closets and it took a little time.

"When I rushed downstairs I found Mrs. Jacobson in the hall telephoning for the police. She fainted just as she hung up the receiver, and I picked her up and carried her into the drawing room and tried to revive her. It was then that I looked up and saw the old gentleman."

"What old gentleman?"

"Sorry. Running a little ahead of myself, I guess. But there he was, just standing there watching me chafe Mrs. Jacobson's wrists and asking what was the matter."

"Who was he?"

"I haven't any idea. I never saw him before in my life."

"What did he look like?"

"Fairly tall, rather distinguished-looking with silvery white hair and a goatee, dressed in a white drill suit. Like something pre-Civil War off a Southern plantation. Just about that time Mrs. Jacobson came to a little and clutched my arm and said, 'In the library—quick—don't let her get away.'

"So I rushed down the hall toward the library, but I couldn't get the door open. While. I was jerking at it, trying to find a bolt or a lock or a key of some sort, I realized that the man was right behind me. And then suddenly he reached out and grabbed the doorknob away from me and shot a trick bolt of some sort and the door opened. And we went in."

"Yeah, go on."

"Well, you know what we found."

"What did the other man say or do?"

"He didn't say anything. Just looked."

"How?"

"I don't know exactly how to describe it. As if he were trying to cover up any betraying emotion."

"Cover up what? Fear, satisfaction, anger, panic?"

"I don't know. He just stood there looking for a minute. Both of us did. And then he reached down and tried to pick up the gun."

"*Huh?*"

"No, no, don't worry. I didn't let him. I grabbed his arm and jerked him back. He turned on me. Angry. Shook my hand off and started to say something. Something like 'who' or 'what.' Then he must have decided against it, because he turned and rushed from the room."

"Where'd he go?"

"I don't know. He just disappeared. And, frankly, I wasn't paying much attention to him right then. I had other things on my mind."

"Yes, I know. Anyone else in the room?"

"No. There are wide French doors at either end, you know. One of them was open. Anyone who was in the room could easily have slipped out."

"Then why the locked door into the hall?"

"I think Mrs. Jacobson probably did that. In a panic, forgetting about the French doors."

"Yeah. I've got to talk to her."

He gave O'Hara a nod of dismissal, and opened the door into the hall to speak to a uniformed patrolman on duty. "How is she?"

"Coming around. The doc says any time now you want to talk to her it's O. K., only go easy."

When the inspector left Theron O'Hara and crossed the hall to the big drawing room, the police doctor reiterated the admonition. "Weak heart, and it won't stand an awful lot, so handle her with gloves."

The housekeeper was lying on one of the big davenports that flanked a massive fireplace, and she was so small and frail and white that she seemed lost and dwarfed in its overstuffed bosom. Her hair was gray and her hands showed the knotting of long years of work. It was plain that she had suffered a terrific shock and had little strength. The inspector decided to waste as little of it as possible.

"Mrs. Jacobson, I have to ask you a few questions. As far as possible answer just 'Yes' or 'No.' I want to make things as easy as I can for you."

She raised her tired blue eyes to his gratefully.

"About eight o'clock this evening a man named Connery or Conway called at the house?"

"Y-yes. Conrad."

"Ever seen him before or heard of him?"

"No."

"What sort of a looking fellow was he?"

"Dark—medium height—just ordinary."

"Know what he was here for?"

"No."

"How long did he stay?"

"About an hour. I didn't see him go—but I heard his car leave."

"Any other visitors?"

"There was a woman."

"What time did she come?"

No answer.

The inspector looked apprehensively at the doctor and then back at the housekeeper. He repeated the question a little louder.

"She came . . . a little after nine."

"Do you know her name or who she was?"

"No. She just said she had an appointment."

"Had you ever seen her before?"

"No."

"And you showed her into the library?"

"Yes."

"And then what happened?"

"I was told to . . . bring liqueurs. I did and they each took a glass."

"Where were they sitting when you brought the liqueurs?"

"Mr. Steinmark at the desk. The lady in a chair—a little bit to the front and side."

"Then what did you do?"

"I left them alone. And not very long after that . . . the shot."

She paused for strength. Then went on.

"I . . . I rushed into the library. And she was standing there . . . with the gun in her hand. She started toward me to get out the door . . . but I . . . I pushed her back. Back into the room and . . . and I locked the door . . . outside. And then . . . telephoned police. Then Mr. O'Hara came and . . . I guess I fainted."

They waited again. Then the inspector spoke gently. "Mrs. Jacobson, can you tell us what this woman looked like?"

"Lovely-looking—dark hair—tall."

"And how was she dressed?"

"Lilac-colored evening gown . . . with . . . with . . ."

"Never mind, Mrs. Jacobson. That'll be enough for this time." It was the doctor who interrupted. He gave Frye a significant glance and the inspector nodded in acceptance.

"I'll take a look in there," he said, and jerked his head in the direction of the library.

The library was at the rear, reached through a long hall on one side of which was the stairway leading to the second floor. There was a uniformed patrolman now in front of the door, standing guard until all the complicated apparatus of photographers and fingerprint men and ballisticians could arrive.

The inspector nodded briefly to him and entered the room. It was a long room with wide French doors at either end. Those at the east end were open and there was a patrolman outside. The inspector stepped carefully through the open French doors onto the stone flagging of a terrace that led to a hard graveled driveway.

He regarded the stone and the gravel regretfully. If the lady in lilac had left through this door there was little chance of a revealing footprint. And it seemed quite likely that she had, for the French doors at the other end of the library had been found closed.

On the other side of the driveway was a narrow strip of lawn and then a dense stretch of trees and shrubbery. The inspector and his men had searched it carefully when they had first come, but had found nothing. Beyond it and at some distance was a large, untenanted house.

Frye reentered the library and strode its length to the closed French doors at the west end and peered out into the dark. They gave directly onto the grass. A detective was already at work with a flashlight on the green carpet of the lawn, but the inspector was not too sanguine. He noted mentally that both pairs of doors—the one at the east, which had been open, and the one at the west, which had been closed—were flanked by heavy shrubbery.

He turned his attention from the closed doors to the long room. The furnishings were baroque in their richness. Heavy brocade hangings, Persian rugs, intricate carvings. A fireplace of some strange mosaic. Lush. Too lush. Theatrical even, as if it were a stage set rather than a room to be lived in.

There was a table desk of elaborately inlaid woods in the center of the room, and a single lamp of hammered Byzantine brass cast a circle of light that was caught and broken into iridescent fragments by two crystal liqueur glasses.

On the desk there was a square of heavy white note paper headed by an address, and across it sprawled a brief letter. "Dear Miss Starr—I will see you Thursday evening about . . ."

And beside the desk was the body of Hugo Steinmark.

Inspector Frye noted the position of the body, the placing of the chairs. He pulled an old envelope from his pocket, made a rough sketch and surveyed it thoughtfully.

Yeah, that was it. Hugo Steinmark sitting at the desk with his back to the north. The "lady in lilac" in the chair to the front and side with her back to the south.

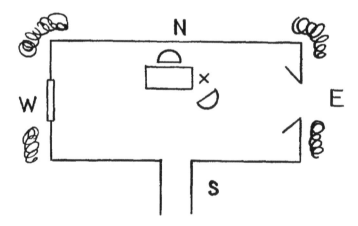

The body had fallen half forward, half sideways. It lay now somewhat on the left side. A bullet had entered the left breast. The gun was still on the floor at one side.

The inspector bent closer and looked at Hugo Steinmark.

A big man, but not fat. Lean, even, and well proportioned. The most striking feature was a heavy Van Dyke beard trimmed to an imperious point that gave the skin by contrast an almost ivory pallor. About the temples. there was the slight graying that comes with the middle forties.

Not even the inevitable sag of death could rob the mouth of its character. Large, mobile, sensitive—and extremely shrewd. The mouth of a man who knew how to combine art and the cash register. A handsome man, a ruthless man perhaps; a man who seemed somehow to fit into the high theatricalism of death and murder.

Inspector Frye did not touch the body nor the heavy brown stain that spread sideways across the white shirt front onto the floor. But he looked for a long time at the thing clutched in the dead man's outflung hand.

A torn piece of chiffon, fuchsia, splashed with purple pansies.

6

Joanna Starr looked out of the bathroom window.

Twenty floors up. And a stiff wind blowing from the north. That was good. That would blow the smoke away quickly. She wondered if it would make much, the lilac dress there in the bathtub, the slippers and the velvet jacket and the torn bit of fuchsia chiffon splashed with purple pansies.

Her hands were steady now, but still cold. The panic of the night was gone, and in its place there was hard caution backed by hard thinking.

She had thought a long time about the lilac dress. She couldn't take it with her. She couldn't take a bag. She'd heard about people walking out of hotels with bags. There were other people who stopped you, questioned whether you were trying to skip out without paying your bill. Or was that only in small country hotels? She didn't know.

She could make a bundle of the lilac dress. But it would still be with her. The incriminating link. It would have to be disposed of sometime, somewhere. And she didn't know where she was going. Just away, as far as she could get.

She'd been right not to leave the hotel in the middle of the night. It might have been conspicuous. Much better to wait for the early morning traffic in hall and elevator and lobby so that she could slip into its stream and be lost.

But she must not wait too long. She must not give them too much time to trace down the two taxi drivers. Even in the panic of flight the previous night some vestiges of craft and cunning had remained with her. She had taken a cab east from Shore Road into the maze of South Brooklyn. Then changed to another and doubled back to Manhattan.

She looked at her watch. Seven o'clock. Seven-fifteen would be about right. That would just give her time to burn the stuff in the bathtub, clear up the refuse. She struck a match, held it to the delicate fabric of the dress, and a little curl of flame crept along a hand-felled seam.

For the hundredth time she checked over in her mind the events of the previous night, making sure that her reasoning was sound. She hadn't given her name. There were only the clothes to identify her. Only a description. Young woman, dark hair and eyes, tall, dressed in a lilac satin dress trimmed with fuchsia and carrying part of a fuchsia handkerchief.

That troubled her, that handkerchief, the other half of it torn somehow from the crystal bracelet at her wrist. They'd find that, and trace it.

Smoke curled up from the bathtub, drifted out the window, and she choked slightly. She snatched a heavy bath towel from a rack over the tub to keep it from the flames licking upward along the lilac seams. She went into the bedroom and closed the door behind her.

The first awful terror of the night was over. Hysteria and tears were luxuries she could no longer afford. Every nerve now was taut, poised, alert. She looked out of the bedroom window to the left toward the bathroom. There was a little smoke, but the wind was dissipating it quickly.

The sound at the door jerked her up sharply. The door leading into the hall. Not the bell, but a knock. Soft, discreet. For a moment she stood perfectly still, made no sound. The knock came again. A little louder this time.

Perhaps—perhaps it was just the maid. Wanting to come in to do the room, trying to find out whether she was there. Trying not to waken her if she were asleep. Knocking softly instead of using the bell. Yes, that was it, she reassured herself. The maid.

She glanced quickly toward the bathroom door. There was a tiny curl of smoke showing near the sill. She grabbed the bathtowel from the bed where she had flung it, and hastily banked it up against the crack at the foot of the door.

Then she crossed the room to the other door leading into the hall and opened it a few inches. "I'll be out in a moment and you can—"

She broke off, fell back. Her hand went up to her throat in a convulsive gesture.

A man pushed open the door and walked into the room and shut it softly behind him.

It was Paul Saniel.

For a moment they just stood there looking at each other. A little bit like that first time. Neither of them said a word. Paul Saniel. She hadn't counted on him. She hadn't included him in her considerations, in her careful checking and planning. She had forgotten about him.

And now, here he was. Standing there. Staring at her. Staring at her in that same blank, expressionless way. And then the blank façade cracked into a sardonic smile.

"Up rather early, aren't you? Didn't you sleep well last night?"

"I—" She started to speak, but the words wouldn't come. There weren't any words. Her new-found coolness and calculating calm had left her.

"Or perhaps you were just going?" He noted her hat and coat. "A week end in the country?"

A week end in the country. Silly. But a straw. She grabbed onto it.

"Yes. Yes, I'm leaving any minute now."

His eyes swept the room again. "Without a bag?"

"I was—I was just going to pack." The closet door was on her right. She fumbled for the knob, trying to appear casual. Her hand pulled a suitcase from the shelf. She flung it onto the bed, opened a dresser drawer.

He still just stood there. Like a cat playing with a mouse. She felt a desire to scream.

"I'm—terribly busy, just now. I have some—some telephoning to do. I can't talk to you now. Please run along. I'll give you a ring when I get back to town and we'll—" The words petered out. Silly words any, way. And he wasn't paying any attention.

He had settled himself in a chair, dragging it over so that it blocked the door. He was pulling out a newspaper. Not a fresh newspaper, but crumpled and folded as if it had already been read once. His face was hidden behind it now.

"I see by the papers," he said, and there was a conscious nonchalance in his voice as if he were remarking the weather or the time of day, "I see by the papers that Hugo Steinmark was murdered last night."

For a moment her breath caught in her throat and she felt again the clutch of panic. Then some inner mentor cracked out orders. Quick! Act! Act for all you're worth! As you never did before, on stage or off

She fell back a step, shocked. "Hugo Stein— What did you say?"

"Murdered," he repeated with relish. "The papers are full of it. And the police are looking for a man named Conrad and an elderly Southern colonel and a tall, dark, beautiful woman. 'The lady in lilac,' they call her. It seems the housekeeper gave a description and—" He broke off, coughed, pulled out a handkerchief and wiped his blinking eyes.

"Here, give me that paper." She tried to snatch it from him. She choked. Out of the corner of her eye she darted a glance at the bathroom door. There were little trails of smoke around the margins of the bath towel. The wind must have changed. Blowing it back into the room.

He put down the paper and rose slowly from his chair. His eyes had followed her quick, darting glance to the bathroom door. Then they flashed back to her. Again the derisive, sardonic smile.

"You're not by any chance trying to burn up that lovely lilac dress of yours, are you?" He strode across the room and opened the door and walked into the smoke-filled bathroom.

For a wild moment she thought of slamming the bathroom door, locking him in, making a dash for it.

"Very wise of you." He reappeared in the doorway. "Only I took the liberty of rescuing—this." He waved the torn piece of fuchsia handkerchief. "A memento." And very carefully he folded it and stuck it in his breast pocket.

She could feel her heart pounding. She must say something, do something. She started to speak, but he held up his hand.

"Sorry, but there's really nothing you can say, you know. We'll just stay here until the fire is over so we can gather up the ashes and the charred bits of heel brilliants, and clean up the bathtub, and then we'll leave. For a week end in the country."

She stared at him. "'We'?" she said.

"Yes: You and I. You're coming with me."

"And—and if I refuse?"

He shrugged his shoulders. "In that case it will be the easiest thing in the world for me to tell the police where their 'lady in lilac' is to be found. And to give them this." He patted the pocket where he had put the torn handkerchief. "Finish packing and I'll strap up the suitcase for you."

Her eyes wavered, dropped. And fell upon the suitcase on the bed. Heavy brown leather. *Take care of it—I mean the heavy brown one. You may need it someday. Need it badly.*

The words came back to her, intruding foolishly. What had they to do with her now? What had anything to do with her now? Anything but that man last night. Dead at her feet. And this other man, here this morning, weaving a net around her, forging a trap, buckling the straps of a suitcase.

And now for the first time since horror had paralyzed her mind and erased from it everything but the imperative demands of the present, she thought of that other Joanna.

Had she known . . .

7

Mrs. Jacobson was better.

A sedative and a trained nurse furnished by the police department had conspired successfully to bring her a refreshing night's rest. Now she was back in the drawing room, propped up in an easy chair while Inspector Frye paced the rug in front of her.

"Let me get this straight," he was saying. "Last night there was no one else in the house but you, Mr. Steinmark, Mr. Theron O'Hara and the other servants?"

"That's right."

"Where was Mrs. Steinmark?"

"She—she was next door. Over there." She gestured toward the open window.

The inspector knew the layout. Evergreen Drive in spite of its imposing name was only a secluded dead end street leading off from Brooklyn's Shore Road. Along one side of the street there were heavily wooded lots. Three widely separated houses stood on the other side.

Hugo Steinmark's was the center house. It was set well back, half hidden from the drive by trees and shrubbery. In front was a wide, carefully landscaped lawn, but pressing in close on the other three sides were dense trees. There was an untenanted house on the east. A gable of the house on the west could be seen at some distance through the foliage.

"Who lives there?"

"Mr. Kingston. He's Mrs. Steinmark's father."

"And she was spending the night with him last night?"

"Well . . . yes."

"Why do you hesitate?"

"Well, that isn't quite so. I mean to say she's . . . she doesn't live here any more."

"Oh, I see. You mean she and Mr. Steinmark have separated?"

"I . . . I think so."

"When?"

"Just a few days ago. Sunday it was. She left the house and took her personal belongings with her."

"Has she been back since?"

There was no answer and the inspector had to repeat the question. "Has she?"

The housekeeper's hands pleated the belt of her dressing gown nervously. "She was here . . . last night."

The inspector's eyebrows went up. Here was a fish he hadn't really been angling for. He had been under the impression that the "lady in lilac" was the only female visitor the previous night.

"Just when last night?"

"I don't like telling this but . . . but I suppose I must."

"That's right. You must."

"Well, it was a little after nine. A little after that other one had arrived, the one in the lilac dress. I had showed her into the library. She and Mr. Steinmark were alone in the library when Mrs. Steinmark came to the house."

"What did she want?"

"She has always been very . . . jealous. I think she must have been watching this house from that one over there."

"You mean she saw the 'lady in lilac' come?"

"Yes. And she wanted to know who the woman was. She was determined to go into the library. She got very insistent, but finally I was able to . . . to persuade her to leave."

"Persuade? Tell me, how big a woman is Mrs. Steinmark?"

"Above average in height and she's fairly heavy."

"And I'll bet you don't weigh a hundred. What did you use? Ju-jitsu?"

"No, I just . . . I mean I usually was able to manage her."

"'Manage'? You mean she—"

"No, no! Not that exactly. It's just that she's very quick-tempered and flies into rages, and she's very— She's not very well balanced emotionally. I think that's one reason why Mr. Kingston built his house so close by."

"I see. You mean he wanted to keep an eye on her. He wanted—"

Before he could develop this idea, there, fortuitously and inexplicably, was a man, striding along a flagstone path toward the Steinmark house, his silvery-white hair waving in the wind and the folded newspaper he held in his hand exploding in loud reports as he beat it angrily against the white drill of his suit.

He didn't pause to ring the bell or to wait for the escort of a servant. He marched into the hall and brushed past the patrolman on duty.

"Where," he demanded in a loud, booming voice, "is this infernal Inspector Frye?"

Before the patrolman could protest either the intrusion or the aspersion, the door from the drawing room opened.

"Who wants to know?" the inspector demanded.

"Oh, so you're the one, are you? You're the one who has broadcast to the newspapers that I am 'wanted by the police.' Like a common criminal."

"Just who are you?"

The intruder made a deep, formal bow and his lips curled with irony. "Douane Kingston—at your service. It was not necessary, my dear sir, to turn the police and press loose on my trail. I came, I assure you, as soon as I read the shocking columns of this morning's news." And he flourished the folded paper before the inspector's nose.

The inspector's jaw tightened. "Mr. Kingston, I'd like to ask you a few questions. Would you mind stepping into this little anteroom?"

"I certainly would. Anything you have to say to me, or I to you, will have to be in the presence of witnesses, pending the arrival of my attorney. Although I must say that I hardly relish the idea of depending on one of your colleagues—or shall I say conspirators?— for the impartiality of observation that the circumstances—"

"Mr. Kingston!" The inspector cut through sharply. "Were you at this house last night?"

"So you're setting traps, are you? Trying to—"

"Were you at this house last night or weren't you?"

"I . . . ah . . . yes."

"When?"

"I arrived here very soon after my son-in-law was murdered. You know that already, so why do you pretend that it is necessary to extract the information from me?"

"Never mind about that. What did you come here for?"

Kingston hesitated. "I—I was looking for my daughter. Shortly after dinner she confessed the need of a little air and said she was going out for a walk. As time went on I felt that the stroll was unduly prolonged and I took a walk myself in search of her."

"And what made you search here? I understand your daughter and Mr. Steinmark had separated."

"My dear man, I cannot be held accountable for the fallacies of your understanding. If you elect to jump to erroneous conclusions, to credit irresponsible sources, to—"

"Were they separated, or weren't they?"

"They . . . ah . . . yes."

"All right, then. Go on. You came here looking for your daughter. What happened?"

"I came in the front door and found a strange man in the drawing room trying to revive Mrs. Jacobson. I accompanied him to the library, where we discovered my son-in-law. Then I left."

"Where'd you go?"

"Home naturally. Under the circumstances I was somewhat shaken. I am not in the habit of stumbling over dead bodies."

"And where was your daughter all this time?"

Again the slight hesitation. "She . . . she had preceded me apparently. She was home when I got there."

"And was she . . . somewhat shaken, too?"

Kingston drew himself up. "Are you insinuating by any chance that my daughter knew anything of the murder of her husband until I myself told her this morning? Are you suggesting that—"

"Yes. That's exactly what I'm suggesting. Did she?"

"Certainly not. When I arrived she was already on her way to bed. She bade me good night in the hall and went to her room, calm and serene, unconscious of the frightful tragedy."

"Well, if she was so calm and serene, why didn't you tell her then instead of waiting until this morning?"

"Because my daughter is of a nervous and excitable disposition, and her recent domestic trials have—"

"I thought you said she was calm and serene?"

"She was—last night."

"But not this morning?"

"Would you be calm if you had just been informed of the murder of a near relative?"

"So what happened when you told her?"

"Under the circumstances what would you expect to happen? She is completely shattered."

"Why'd she leave her husband?"

"That, my dear sir, is a subject I would prefer not to discuss—with you."

"Very well, I'll discuss it with her."

Sudden alarm routed austere dignity. "No . . . no you can't do that."

"Why not?"

"Because . . . I . . . she . . ." He strode quickly to the door as if he would bar the inspector's way. "I told you my daughter was prostrated. She's in no condition to . . . to . . ." His agitation increased. Suddenly he jerked the door open and was gone, hurrying down the flagstone path toward that other house beyond the trees.

The inspector stood for a moment watching him, puzzled, grim. He couldn't decide whether it was an act or whether . . . He wondered.

He summoned a patrolman, gave him a few curt orders and watched him as he disappeared in the direction of the Kingston house. Then he turned and went back to the housekeeper in the drawing room. He pulled out a notebook in which he had penciled a timetable.

"I'd like to check this with you, Mrs. Jacobson. I couldn't last night because you were too done in. I want to get perfectly clear the list of visitors here last night. First there was Mr. O'Hara for dinner. Then this Mr. Conrad. After him the lady, the one in lilac. And while she was here, Mrs. Steinmark. Is that correct?"

"Yes, that's right. Only there was one more."

"*Huh?*"

"There was another man came. I suppose I should have told you about it before, but it seems like my brain doesn't work all of a piece since last night. I remember everything pretty clear, but in bits. There was someone else after Mrs. Steinmark."

"After she had left and the other woman, the one in the lilac dress, was still in the library with Mr. Steinmark, the front bell rang and I answered it. It was a young man, a nice-looking fellow. He didn't give any name. He just said he wanted to see Mr. Steinmark. I told him that Mr. Steinmark was engaged for the moment. But he said he wouldn't wait. And he went away."

"Away where?"

"I don't know. I didn't notice."

"Was he on foot or did he have a car?"

"I don't know. The drive is hidden from the house by the shrubbery. But a few minutes later I was in the kitchen and I heard . . ."

8

But while puzzling angles were piling up at the Steinmark house, headquarters solved at least one of the previous night's quota.

Detective Homer in the inspector's office could not, however, take much credit, for the plum fell into his lap, or rather walked into the office in the person of a dark-haired man of medium height in the indeterminate middle thirties.

"The name," he said, "is Konrad—with a K. Not C, as you have it in the papers. Jules Konrad." And he laid the morning paper he was carrying on the detective's desk. He smiled slightly.

"I just read that I was 'wanted by the police' and I came right over. I'm the man who called on Hugo Steinmark last night just before he was murdered."

He was, he said, a lawyer and he gave the address of his Broad Street office. He had gone last night to see Hugo Steinmark on behalf of a client.

"Was it usual," the detective interrupted, "for Steinmark to transact business after hours at his home in Brooklyn instead of during the day at his office in New York?"

"No, I don't suppose so. But, you see, my business was not usual, and I think he preferred to discuss it in the privacy of his own home."

"What was it?"

"I am representing Trudi Hess, the film actress who arrived in New York a few days ago from Hollywood. Under ordinary circumstances I would not discuss a client's affairs with the police.

But these are not ordinary circumstances. My client, Trudi Hess, was—" He broke off, then came out with it. "She was Hugo Steinmark's wife."

Detective Homer's eyebrows lifted. "I wasn't aware that he had been married before."

"You were not supposed to be aware of it."

"He has been married to his present wife about ten years. When was he divorced from the first one?"

"He was not divorced."

"You mean he was a bigamist?"

"Exactly. And his name was not really Hugo Steinmark, you know. It was August Steiner. It was under that name that he married Trudi Hess in Graz, Austria, fifteen years ago. They were in the same theatrical company. He deserted her a year later and came to America and she never heard from him again. Here in the United States he took a new name and became a famous producer. It was the documentary proof of all this that I showed him last night."

"How'd he take it?"

Konrad laughed a little. "I hardly have words to describe it. He denied it, of course, at first. But after he saw the proofs I had, he knew the game was up. He was—well, flabbergasted is a little mild. He was so sure that he'd covered all his tracks, that no one would ever connect the great Hugo Steinmark of America with the obscure provincial actor of Austria. And it was on the second Mrs. Steinmark's money, you know, that he built up the producing organization behind his fortune."

"And I suppose Trudi Hess was after her share of it."

"To the contrary. My client is very well off in her own right. She was merely seeking reconciliation. Now, of course, she will lay claim to the Steinmark estate."

Detective Homer leaned back and regarded the man before him. Here was a mouthful. The last person but one to see Hugo Steinmark alive, presenting him with the proofs of bigamy.

"Tell me again just what time you went to the Steinmark house."

"My appointment was for eight and I think I was on time, although I didn't notice particularly."

"And how long were you with him?"

"Three quarters of an hour perhaps."

"What did he propose to do about what you had just told him?"

"I don't think he knew himself. He asked me for time to think it over, and said he would call me today at my office."

Detective Homer was thoughtful for a moment.

"Of course you understand, Mr. Konrad, that since you are one of the people who were at the Steinmark house last night we will have to ask you for a very careful account of your actions after you left there."

"Certainly. It was about a quarter to nine when our interview was over. I left as I had come, by the front door. One of the servants had showed me in, but I didn't see her when I left. My car was parked in the driveway and I drove home in it."

He paused to give the detective the address of his New York apartment.

"Traffic was a bit snarled over the bridge and I drove slowly anyway, so I imagine it was an hour or more before I got back to Manhattan. The garage where I keep my car—it's just a block from my apartment—could tell you better than I. They have some kind of checking system there." He gave the garage's address.

"I really didn't pay much attention to time, for I had no other engagements for that evening. I went to bed early, around eleven I should say, and this morning when I woke up and read the paper I found I was 'wanted by the police.' So . . ."

"You have the documents you showed Steinmark?"

"Not with me just now. They're in the safe in my office. I left them there this morning before I came here. If you'd like to send someone down, though, I'd be only too glad . . ."

But Jules Konrad was not the only surprising visitor that Detective Homer had that morning. Even as he was digesting the implications of the lawyer's revelations and, in the absence of his chief, setting in motion the elaborate checking technique of the police department, another angle of the case was maturing.

In the dining room of the home of Charles W. Newberger, wealthy clothing manufacturer, to be exact. A beautiful dining room, gay with sunshine and chintz, bearing the imprint of a skillful decorator. The whole house was that way, as if there had been a conscious effort to capture and hold light and cheer and sun and hope.

Conscious effort—and wasted effort. Over all the brightness, impervious to clever tricks of color and design and arrangement, lay despair, like a pall, pressing down, invading, permeating. Around the woman sitting across the breakfast table from her husband it was like a tangible, visible aura.

A silent meal broken occasionally by a gentle word, a solicitous inquiry from the man. Words and inquiries that sometimes weren't even answered by the woman. Only when he rose to go did she seem to become concerned with his presence. She clung to him with hands that were frail and white.

"Charles, where are you going? Why are you leaving me? Charles!"

"Just to the office, my dear." His voice was low, patient.

"If I telephone you at eleven will you be there? Will you talk to me at eleven if I telephone you?"

"Well, no, not then. Make it a little later. I'm not going directly to the office."

"Charles, where are you going?" Her eyes went wide and she grabbed his lapels. "Charles, you're seeing *them?* Have you heard from them? Have they got— Oh, Charles, get him back . . . Ronnie . . ."

She clung to him and her body quivered with great shaking sobs. He held he tenderly with one arm, but with the other he reached for a bell. A white-capped nurse appeared and led her away.

His shoulders slumped with an infinite, despairing weariness and he dropped back into his chair. He poured himself another cup of coffee and sipped it idly, his eyes staring before him, hopeless, bitter. Presently the nurse reappeared and sat down at the table and started to eat her breakfast.

He turned to her. "Miss Dunne, at times like this wouldn't it be better to tell her the truth? If she knew it was over, done with, that there wasn't any more hope, it might break through the fogs of hallucination."

"I'm afraid, Mr. Newberger, the doctor would have to decide that."

As Charles W. Newberger got into the limousine waiting in front of his house he gave the chauffeur an address and then settled back with the morning paper. Halfway downtown he changed his orders abruptly.

"Police headquarters," he snapped.

And so it was that, shortly after Jules Konrad left, Detective Homer had another visitor.

"I just read of it in the paper a few minutes ago," the visitor explained, "and I came here immediately. I don't know whether what I have to tell you is relevant or not. That will be for you to decide. But here it is. Six days ago—that would be last Saturday morning—Steinmark telephoned me and asked me to be at his house at eleven o'clock this morning."

"You knew him?"

"No. I'd heard of him of course. Who hasn't? But I never saw him in my life."

"Did he say what he wanted to see you about?"

"No."

"But you made the appointment anyway?"

Newberger nodded.

"Isn't that rather unusual? Making an appointment with a perfect stranger to discuss unspecified business?"

"Yes, I know. Ordinarily a busy man such as I am doesn't pay any attention to such requests. But there was something in his voice, his manner. I don't know exactly what, but I said I'd be there. And then, you see, I always think that perhaps—"

He broke off and the look of bitterness and despair settled upon him again.

The detective reached for a pencil and paper. "You'll let me have your name, please."

"Certainly. Newberger. Charles W. Newberger of number—"

The detective's pencil jerked to a stop and he looked up. "Are you the Charles W. Newberger whose infant son was kidnaped and murdered last year?"

9

Paul Saniel and the girl who called herself Joanna Starr faced each other across a pine table that supported a dim kerosene lamp and the remains of a meal. Through the cabin door came soft night sounds as hills and woods settled into darkness. It was hours now since together they had walked out of the Waldorf-Astoria.

"And quietly without any rumpus, or else . . ." he had said, and his hand had been around her arm and he had leaned forward slightly as he spoke to her. And smiled and carried her suitcase, the heavy brown leather one. And those passing by had been fooled into thinking him only a devoted escort. They hadn't known the steel of his grasp, the threat of his words.

He had a car waiting on a side street and they had driven through the tangled traffic of Manhattan into the Holland Tunnel and out onto the Jersey highways. At first they had pursued a crazy course as if he were deliberately making a difficult trail. At a wayside diner they had stopped for lunch, and after that he had driven with more direction and purpose. West and then north into the hills.

The houses had grown fewer, the hills steeper, the road narrower and without paving, and presently they had stopped at a remote village store and bought supplies and then continued on up into the low-lying mountains.

The cabin was hidden away at the end of an abandoned road overgrown with brambles and strewn with rocks. A neat little cabin in spite of the obvious fact that it had not been used for a long time. The door had been locked, but he had broken the lock. Three rooms, furnished in wicker and homespun, comfortable in spite of dust and an occasional veiling of cobwebs.

They had opened the windows and aired it out and cleaned it and put the supplies in place, and when night had settled down he had cooked supper. A good supper, too. Bacon and eggs, coffee, cheese, melons. And all the time they had spoken scarcely a word.

Occasionally he gave a direction. She asked a brief question. That was all. Tense. Unreal.

And now the empty plates were between them and the kerosene lamp cast a feeble circle of light.

He lit a cigarette and blew a long cloud of smoke. He leaned forward on his arms and his eyes met hers. There was in them none of the smoldering anger of that first encounter in the Rainbow Room. He was hard and calm now—and infinitely more menacing.

"Suppose," he said, "we do some horse trading. Two nights ago I asked you where Joanna Starr was and you refused to tell me. Now I'm asking you again. Where is she?"

She didn't answer at once; but she felt again that stiffening of the nerves, that tautness of the muscles under the necessity for swift, clear thinking.

That same question. Where is she? She had held him off before with bluff, but it wouldn't work again. Too much had happened since then. Then she had only to defend the real Joanna. Now she herself was vulnerable. Then she had been only an impostor. Now. . . .

Tell him! Don't be a fool! Tell him Jason *Restaurants, Unit 7.* What did she owe the real Joanna now? Now after last night. The real Joanna had betrayed her; had given her a name inextricably bound up with something dark and frightful; had played upon her ambition, her spirit and her pride and trapped her.

But had she? At least knowingly? *You get everything you want. Excitement, thrills—danger maybe.* The real Joanna had warned her. Challenged her, too, but warned her just the same. And she had accepted the challenge, made the bargain.

The trouble was she didn't *know.* She didn't know anything. She was like someone walking in the dark, crashing into unknown objects, clutched by cold bruising fingers, stumbling, groping.

She didn't know whether the real Joanna had trapped her or had herself been trapped. She didn't know who Paul Saniel was and what he was to that other girl. But most of all she didn't know whether Hugo Steinmark—

Her thoughts broke and shattered again against the inexplicable horror of that distant room and the man dead at her feet.

"I'm waiting." Paul Saniel's voice snatched her back from the Steinmark library to the little cabin in the mountains. "I'm waiting for you to answer my question. And if the answer is satisfactory I might give you this." He patted the coat pocket which held the torn bit of fuchsia chiffon with a significant gesture.

Horse trading! A bribe! That was it.

Again she made no answer, but her mind was working faster now. He was willing to surrender the one link that bound her to the murder of Hugo Steinmark if she would tell him where Joanna Starr was. But why do it that way?

The forty-eight hours since that, night in the Rainbow Room had dealt him new and infinitely better cards. Aces this time. All aces. He had only to go to the nearest police station and turn over her and the fuchsia handkerchief and she'd be in for it.

She would be in for it, but then so would— She broke off a little breathlessly at the thing she had stumbled onto. All at once she realized that he didn't have all the aces. She still had one. Not the same one, to be sure, that she had held that night in the Rainbow Room. But capable perhaps of taking a trick.

She extracted a cigarette from the pack on the table and lit it slowly, deliberately, to prove to herself and to him the steadiness of her hand.

"I'm afraid," she said, "it's too late for that."

"Rather a *non sequitur*. I don't get it."

"It's too late for us to be horse trading. At least with the horses you suggest. You see, if you were to consign me and that bit of handkerchief to the police, there'd be questions asked about Joanna Starr. And about you."

She paused, watching him closely.

"Tuesday night she was just someone you were searching for. Now she's all bound up with murder. Whether you like it or not.

And if the fuchsia handkerchief and I get involved with the police, she gets involved. And you do, too."

His response was disconcerting. He smiled slightly with patronizing contempt. She hadn't expected that. Nor his head nodding in confirmation of what she had just said.

"Of course. Don't you suppose I had all that figured out? What do you suppose I snatched you away from the police for?"

She stared at him. So he was two jumps ahead of her.

"All right, then. What *did* you do it for?"

"Because—" He broke off, and his eyes narrowed slightly as he contemplated the burning end of his cigarette. "Because I thought perhaps you and I might settle things between ourselves. Quietly. Understand?"

She nodded knowingly. But she didn't really understand anything but the surface implications of his words. That was the whole trouble. She was so vulnerable, so defenseless in her ignorance. Stumbling again in the dark, afraid of making a false step. Not daring to cut through the black fog with truth. For she didn't know what disaster—to her and to the other Joanna—lay on the other side of truth. And so once more she retreated ingloriously into the temporary refuge of hard, stubborn silence.

He read her resolve in the hardening line of her mouth, shrugged his shoulders and rose from the table. He moved slowly, clearing up the dishes.

"There's no hurry," he said in that hard, sardonic voice. "Think it over."

From that moment forward she could feel his eyes always on her, although she could never catch him at it. Even while he was looking at something else, he was still watching her. Never once did she feel herself out of his sight. Never once free from the oppression of his vigilance. It was like handcuffs on her wrists, hobbles on her ankles, a paralyzing hand on her will. She could not, she dared not, rebel. She could only submit.

Once during the night she awakened and looked at her watch, and it was two o'clock. She went to the door leading into the central room and opened it quietly, a tiny crack; and he was there, the couch on which he was sleeping rolled up in front of her door. Or was he sleeping? He did not stir, and in the moonlight she could see his closed eyes. But she still felt their watchfulness.

On the afternoon of the second day they drove to the village for supplies. She didn't want to go. She protested. But he only laid his hand on her arm and said, "Come along," and she knew that resistance would turn gentleness to steel.

He bought a great pile of New York papers in the village store and when they got back to the cabin he read them one by one, sprawled out under a tree, while she sat at a distance on a stone slab that formed the stoop of the cabin.

Presently he rose and came over and sat down beside her. "Maybe," he said, and, she didn't like the curve of his lip or the irony of his tone, "maybe you'd be interested in this." And he handed her the paper he had been reading.

She took it and her eyes tried to concentrate on the blackness of the type and the jumble of headlines. She knew what was there. Murder, and the "lady in lilac" and perhaps a picture of Hugo Steinmark stretched out there on the floor.

"It doesn't upset you, does it?" His voice broke in, cool and derisive.

She didn't answer because plainly he didn't expect an answer. Her eyes followed the lines of type. There was something about a gun—and fingerprints. Of course. Fingerprints were always important in murder cases. That's why people wore gloves. But she hadn't worn gloves.

> Police have not yet been able to trace the official ownership of the gun found beside Steinmark's body, but fingerprints on the liqueur glass handled by the "lady in lilac" corresponded with those on the gun.

Her fingerprints!

> . . . that the identity of the "lady in lilac" has been definitely established as that of a woman named Joanna Starr, who has been registered at the Waldorf-Astoria since Friday, May 29. The six days prior

to that she was registered at the Franconia, a much smaller hotel on East Thirty-first Street. According to information volunteered by the management of a large apartment building on West Eighty-seventh Street, a Joanna Starr had a furnished apartment there for more than a year but left two weeks ago without giving a forwarding address.

The first clue to the identity of the "lady in lilac" came from Miss Meta Bernard, clerk at Bergdorf, Goodman, who identified the scrap of chiffon found clutched in the dead hand of Steinmark as part of a lilac evening costume which she had sold to a Joanna Starr on Wednesday and delivered to the Waldorf. Another clerk at Saks Fifth Avenue . . .

They had been quick about it, identifying the chiffon handkerchief and following its trail to the hotel. She had expected that. Her eyes returned to the paper.

. . . ransom money delivered on September 14 last year to the Grand Central checkstand by Charles W. Newberger. The Newberger child was never returned and its dead body was subsequently discovered in a Long Island swamp near Sayville. The serial number on the $500 bill passed at Bergdorf, Goodman, indicates that it was part of the $50,000 paid out by Newberger. The police are working on the theory that the Joanna Starr stopping at the Waldorf and making purchases in stores is the one who . . .

Her breath came quickly in a little gasp! *Part of the $50,000 paid out by Newberger.*

Fifty thousand dollars! But that was the exact amount of the great wad of bills that the other Joanna had forced upon her! And all of them in denominations of five hundred dollars! . . . *kidnap ransom money . . . and its dead body was subsequently discovered in a . . .*

A shudder of horror and revulsion went through her.

"Nice people I'm going around with," she heard a voice say. "Kidnaping and murder and then more murder. Nice people."

She got up from the stoop and stumbled down the path to the rutted, overgrown road. She could feel his eyes following her. She was trying to think. To think back to that night in the stifling little room under the roof and that other girl seeking the ultimate, tragic release of death.

She could hear her now. *Why didn't you let me go, let me get out of the whole awful, dirty mess?*

She dropped down onto a rough boulder beside the road and began reading again.

> . . . the housekeeper told the police. She described the visitor as tall dark, very good-looking, wearing a rough brown tweed suit. "And then just a few minutes later," Mrs. Jacobson continued, "I was out in the kitchen and I heard a sound outside. The kitchen wing is at the west side of the house and I could look right out the window to the French doors at the west end of the library. It was getting a little dark, but I could see someone crouching there beside the French doors. He was peering through the glass, half hidden by the shrubbery, but I could see it was the same young man. I called out and said, 'What are you doing there?' and I guess that startled him because he got up and sort of slid away and disappeared in the trees on the west side of the house. I felt pretty uneasy, having a prowler around the house and I thought I ought to tell Mr. Steinmark. But I didn't like to disturb him when he had company. So I just stood there in the kitchen trying to decide what to do. And it wasn't more than five minutes after that that I heard the shot that killed Mr. Steinmark."
>
> In confirmation of the housekeeper's story, the police discovered footprints in the soft earth near

the French doors at the west end of the library, and a small swatch of brown tweed caught on a screw protruding from the door casing, indicating that the prowler, startled by the housekeeper's voice and attempting to slip away quickly, had caught his coat on . . .

The paper slid from her hands. Her eyes stared at a distant line of hills. But she wasn't seeing them. She was seeing again that library, and the heavy desk with the pool of light from the lamp of Byzantine brass, and the French doors at either end.

Her throat felt dry and hot and she fought off the panic that flooded her nerves. Now less than ever could she afford fear.

She clutched a jutting edge of the boulder on which she was sitting, clutched it so fiercely that the sharp rock cut into her palm. But she did not feel it. She dared not feel anything now. Feeling would betray her, tear down her guard, leave her no protection against those watching eyes.

She forced herself to pick up the paper, to go on, to read it all— every column of the Steinmark murder case. The last story ended on page ten beside a department store ad. She came to the bottom of the column and finished off the final paragraph.

Her eyes wandered over the rest of the page. But again she wasn't seeing what she was looking at. She was groping for some coherent pattern, trying to ferret out the relationship between the things she had read and the things she knew without reading.

And yet subconsciously, even while she was thinking, she still continued to read. Mechanical reflex action. Reading without being aware of the words on the page. Until suddenly one thrust itself up into her consciousness. A name. Paul Saniel.

There in the paper before her. On the other side of the department store ad. Totally divorced from the story of the Steinmark murder. Unrelated, independent, under a headline of its own.

INVESTIGATE DISAPPEARANCE
OF DIRECTOR
Police have been asked to hunt for Paul Saniel missing from the Hotel Wessex since early Thursday

morning. A drive-yourself car service reported that Saniel had hired one of their cars, a Chevrolet coupé, number 478932, on Thursday morning but had failed to return it Thursday night in accordance with their twelve hour agreement. Saniel arrived recently from Hollywood, where he is a director for Imperial. His most recent picture is *Dark Danger*, starring Trudi Hess.

She looked up the hill toward the cabin and the car that stood beside it. A Chevrolet coupé. She could see the number quite plainly—478932.

She rose and walked slowly back to the cabin and to the man who was sitting on the stoop. Fear still crept through the dark places of her mind, but she gave no outward sign.

"Did you," she asked, and it was her voice now that was cool and ironic, "did you read *all* of the paper?" And she thrust it at him, folded so that the house-keeper's story stood alone.

She watched him as he read. But his expression never changed. Not even when he had finished and raised his eyes to meet hers. Blank eyes now, like the house with the curtains pulled down.

"Too bad," she said, and took from a peg driven into the rough log of the cabin wall a coat that was hanging there. His coat. Of rough brown tweed. And across the patch pocket on the left front there was a jagged, three-cornered tear.

"Too bad," she repeated, "I haven't a needle and thread, and I'd mend your coat. The New York Police Department might be glad to furnish the patch."

10

"And remember, my child, that you are prostrated. Simply prostrated."

Otto Hess admonished his daughter, and then stood off and surveyed her critically. She was in white, dramatic, startling white. Her blond hair was hidden under a white cowl that hung in long flowing lines over her shoulders, and her gown was a Parisian couturière's version of the White Sister. She wore no jewels. No make-up—if you excepted the shadows above the cheekbones, shadows so skillfully wrought that few would guess that they were synthetic.

There were only her eyes to furnish color. Large and blue like china agates. And wide. Too wide to suit the critical survey of Otto Hess.

"The lids lowered, please. . . . There! That's better. . . . And the head thrown back a little. And remember to walk slowly . . . wearily."

He circled about her like some plump Svengali, a little man, round and pink and well stuffed like an animated wienie.

A maid appeared at the door. "They're waiting."

"Yes, yes, I know." He turned back to this daughter. "And remember too, Trudi, a little more accent. Your English must not be too good," he cautioned, although his own English was excellent with only a slight tinge of alien intonation.

"Yes, Papa." For the first time she spoke, this woman who had thrilled a thousand fans. "I'll remember." Obedient—but bored.

She heaved a deep sigh and let it out slowly, and it was as if boredom and obedience seeped away with the slow exhale and in its place was a woman—prostrated.

The bedroom door was opened at last and Trudi Hess went forth to meet the metropolitan press.

She walked slowly, wearily, her head thrown back in a gesture of noble tragedy; her lids half closed, veiling the grief of her eyes. The hush that fell upon the assemblage was a tribute. A room full of reporters is not easily stilled. Even the semidrunk from the *Gazette*, one of the most scandalous of the scandal sheets, was quiet.

"Gentlemen—I am sorry I have kept you—waiting." Softly, only a little above a whisper as if a long vigil of weeping had robbed her voice of its power. She sank into a chair; rested her forehead on her hand for a moment, shielding her eyes, gaining strength for the ordeal ahead of her.

Behind her a black lacquered screen inlaid with strange mother-of-pearl arabesques threw into somber relief the fluid lines of the white gown, and made a frame for a picture that might have been labeled "Sorrow" in a Burne-Jones frieze.

"You wanted to ask me—questions? Yes?" There was an upward inflection to the "yes."

But one moment of awe is all that the average newspaperman is capable of, particularly when there is a press deadline in the offing. So now after that first instinctive hush, the professional babel of a mass interview broke loose.

"Miss Hess, is it true that . . . Miss Hess, have you . . . Was Hugo Steinmark . . . When did . . . Please, Miss Hess, your face a little to the left. Hold it . . ."

A flash bulb exploded. Another and another.

"But your claim makes a bigamist of Steinmark. You realize that, don't you?" It was the *Gazette* reporter.

She wilted, under the barrage and looked at them in helpless appeal. ("Don't answer individual questions, Trudi," Papa had said. "Just remember your lines, and if you get cornered faint.") "Please, gentlemen, my English is not good. I do not understand always. Just let me tell you—in my own words."

They grew quiet again.

"It was fifteen years ago in Graz, Austria, and . . ."

It was a touching picture of Bohemia in a provincial touring company; of struggling young actors, and great ambitions, and betrayal and disillusion.

"For fifteen years, gentlemen, I have been August Steiner's wife. And then in exile, I longed to see him again. I knew he had gone to America, and so about six months ago I hired a lawyer to find him. When my last picture was finished in Hollywood, there was no word yet of my husband. So I came here.

"Perhaps I could help in the search for him. But when I arrived on Wednesday there was still no word of him. And then yesterday morning Mr. Konrad came with the news that he had found him . . ." She paused, her voice uncertain. ". . . found him and that he was—dead."

She pressed the long chiffon handkerchief to her lips. "That— that is all, gentlemen."

"He has a wife here, you know."

"Yes, yes, I know. I am sorry for her. But mine is the—what do you say?—the prior claim."

"But have you proofs?"

"You mean papers, documents? Yes, yes, of course. Mr. Konrad . . ." She made a vague gesture.

It took Jules Konrad almost half an hour to get from his Broad Street office to the hotel, a half-hour during which Trudi Hess retired to an inner room of her suite. But when the lawyer arrived she returned to the reporters.

The documents were worth waiting for. August Steiner's birth certificate, a wedding license, an application for a passport to America with a photograph, photostats of documents in the American department of immigration.

"How long had you known Steinmark was the man you were after?" one of the reporters asked Konrad.

"I didn't *know* until Thursday night. I had had my suspicions for some days. But they were only suspicions. That's why I didn't impart them to Miss Hess when she arrived here Wednesday. I wanted to make sure first. Well, I made sure Thursday night."

"And what was Steinmark going to do about it all?"

"I don't know precisely. When I showed these documents to him, he denied them at first, then temporized, and then talked of 'secrecy' and a 'settlement.'"

"What kind of a settlement was he prepared to make?"

"I don't know. That isn't what my client was interested in. He asked me to come back for another interview the next day, and naturally I said I would. However . . ." He shrugged his shoulders expressively, for, of course, there had been no "next day" for Hugo Steinmark.

"Did you have any—"

"That'll be all, boys. Scram." A new voice entered the conversation and disrupted it. Inspector Frye of the homicide squad loomed unannounced in the doorway to the suite. "Get going. I've got to talk to Miss Hess alone."

The reporters protested and grumbled from habit as they straggled out of the room. The inspector had said "alone," but apparently he excepted Otto Hess and the lawyer when he sat down to talk to Trudi Hess.

"This," he said, turning to a man who had accompanied him, "is Detective Rochester of the Missing Persons Bureau. Tell me, Miss Hess, do you know a man named Paul Saniel?"

She was still sitting with her back against the lacquered screen. At the sound of the name she straightened slightly. "Why . . . why, yes."

"What do you know about him?"

"Only that he . . ." She hesitated. (Papa hadn't told her what to say about Paul. She didn't have any lines now. And what was it the lawyer had said? "Better soft-pedal anything about this Paul fellow.") "He was my director in Hollywood," she went on.

"You knew him pretty well?"

"Yes . . . pretty well."

"Did you know he was in New York?"

"Why, I . . . uh . . . no."

"Well, he disappeared Thursday morning from the Hotel Wessex. We thought you might have some idea . . ."

She stifled a secret sigh of relief. Was that all? All she had to say was that she hadn't seen him . . . didn't know . . .

"I'm sorry, but I'm afraid I can't help you. I haven't seen P— Mr. Saniel since we finished the picture in Hollywood two weeks ago."

Papa smiled and she knew she had said the right thing.

"Did he have any friends or relatives here in New York?"

She shook her head. "He did not speak of anyone here."

Mr. Konrad smiled and she knew she had said the right thing again.

"Have you any photographs of Saniel?"

"I don't know. I suppose somewhere in the press pictures . . ." She was vague.

The detectives asked to see the press pictures, and Otto Hess brought them from a big portfolio of photographs and clippings. Most of them were devoted to Trudi Hess, but in a number of informal shots of work on the set she shared the spotlight with the director.

"A studio photograph would be better than these stills. You don't have one, do you?" the inspector demanded.

"I . . . no, only just those. No personal photographs."

When the two men from headquarters left they carried three of the stills with them. As the door closed behind them, grief and tragedy slipped from the shoulders of Trudi Hess like the long white cowl that she pushed back from her forehead and sent sliding to the floor.

"Papa, it's hot." Her voice was cross. "Why don't you send out for beer and goose livers with rye bread?"

"No, no, Trudi. You don't dare. You're three pounds over now."

"But, Papa, I'm hungry." Like an irritable child.

"No." The little man was firm. Trudi sulked but finally accepted the ultimatum and changed the subject.

"Did I do all right? Was I—"

"Babe, you were terrific."

Papa's eyes popped out of his head. Trudi's mouth fell open foolishly. Jules Konrad turned with a quick, puzzled frown toward the black lacquered screen. All three of them stared as the man came out from behind it and swayed slightly. It was the *Gazette* reporter.

"Terrific," he repeated. "Collos—"

"What are you doing here?" the lawyer interrupted angrily. "What do you mean by hiding and spying? You've no business—"

"Oh, yes, I have, brother. That's exactly my business. Hiding and spying. You don't suppose I get news like those other punks, do you?" And he gestured derisively toward the door through which the other reporters had left.

"Well, you can get out now. And be quick about it."

"Oh, sure, sure. I never stick around where I'm not wanted—after I get what I want." He grinned. "Such as this. It was on that little stand behind the screen. I guess you must have forgotten about it when the dicks asked you for a personal studio shot." And he held up an elaborately framed photograph with an intimate inscription across the bottom. The signature was *Paul Saniel.*

"Flossy. Very flossy. Tell me, Miss Hess, you and your director weren't by any chance in love with each other or anything like that?"

Trudi Hess stared at him, her eyes wide and china blue now.

"You can answer 'Yes' or 'No,'" he insisted. "Were you?"

"Why, I . . . he . . ."

Suddenly the china blue went into eclipse, veiled by dark lashes. She swayed, uttered a little cry and crumpled to the floor.

And if you get cornered, Trudi, you can always faint.

At the same time another photograph was changing hands down at headquarters, and once again Detective Homer found a plum tossed into his lap.

The police had been struggling with the problem of the "lady in lilac." The descriptions they had received from the Steinmark housekeeper and from clerks in stores were vivid with words, and the words were duly printed in the papers, but a whole column of talk is as nothing compared with one swift flash of a photographer's camera. There were a number of people to tell what Joanna Starr looked like, but no one had a picture of her.

That is, there was no one until Mr. Featheridge made his appearance. Mr. Featheridge had a photographer's shop on the corner of Broadway and Eighty-fourth Street. When he read the name of Joanna Starr in the newspapers he grew thoughtful and began searching his files.

Later at police headquarters he explained things to Detective Homer. "She came in a few weeks before Christmas and I took the photograph. I remember her particularly because she wanted a very special kind of color photograph that gives the effect of a miniature done on ivory. It's delicate work and expensive, but she didn't seem to mind that. In fact, she added to the expense by buying a very lovely gold frame for it. I delivered the job to her two days before Christmas, and I concluded that it was intended as a Christmas gift for someone."

"Was that the only one she had finished?"

"Yes. I always keep all negatives, and this print here I made up only this morning after I decided I ought to show it to the police. She herself last Christmas ordered only one. I thought at the time it was rather queer, because most people order at least half a dozen, though not, of course, a half dozen of the color photographic miniatures that I have just told you about. I got the impression that it was for someone very special."

"Did she say who?"

"No, I just got the impression."

"And this woman was Joanna Starr?"

"That was the name she gave me, and the address to which I delivered the picture two days before Christmas was the West Eighty-seventh Street address that you have. You can always take this photograph to the superintendent there for verification."

Which is exactly what Detective Homer did. It was a huge apartment building and he eyed it skeptically. He would have preferred something small and intimate that facilitated checking on the habits of tenants. This one had eighteen floors and probably two hundred tenants. Inspector Frye, he knew, had already been there, but without any photograph.

The building superintendent was immediately helpful. He looked at the picture and nodded. "Sure, that's her. The woman who used to live here. I told one of your men all about her the other day. She had a furnished apartment, but moved out about two weeks ago."

Two of the elevator boys and a clerk in the rental office backed up his identification, but they could add little to it.

"Nice lady. Never fussed about anything," the super said.

"Always paid prompt," from the clerk.

"Visitors?" The elevator operators raised skeptical eyebrows. "There's one hundred and ninety-six apartments in the building and tenants come and go. It would be hard to keep track."

The telephone operators weren't helpful either, for the switchboard was connected only with the house system. Outside calls were made on private phones in the individual apartments.

And there was no forwarding address.

Nevertheless, Detective Homer felt good. His satisfaction was tempered after he had shown the photograph around a bit.

"No, sir, that's not the one." Mrs. Jacobson was very positive. "The same general type, but that's not the girl that visited Mr. Steinmark."

The attendants at the Waldorf were vague. After all, they did see hundreds of people every twenty-four hours, and most of the guests were room numbers rather than faces.

The clerk at Bergdorf, Goodman backed up Mrs. Jacobson.

But none of these items was quite as choice as the one even then being pounded out by a reporter on a notorious Hollywood scandal sheet.

It was the *Gazette* reporter who was responsible. From the interview with Trudi Hess he had gone back to his paper and reported, and on the basis of that report the managing editor had wired the *Gazette's* Hollywood correspondent.

11

They stood on top of a high cliff, where the road swerved close to a precipitous ledge, and watched the car as it plunged downward, smashing itself to pieces in the ravine below.

With a final echoing crash it bounded from a low bank and settled into the bottom of a dry creek bed, a mass of broken, twisted metal—anonymous metal, for all identifying numbers of chassis and body had been filed away. And the license plates carrying the number 478932 were broken to bits and flung into another ravine.

"So now we walk," he said laconically, and turned and beckoned the girl down the trail in front of him.

She hesitated. "Suppose," she said, "we walk side by side."

"Afraid I might knife you in the back? Is that it?" And he fell in step beside her.

They walked down the trail in silence. Not the gentle, soft silence of wood and mountain and forest that was all around them, but a grim, guarded silence.

The path dropped down and down until they were once more on the rough, unpaved back road that led to the village. It was a tiny place, the kind that natives usually refer to as a "wide place in the road." There was a railroad station, a post office, a general store and a drugstore where they sold newspapers.

At the door of the drugstore she stopped. "I'll stay outside. You go on in."

He hesitated uncertainly.

She laughed and her voice was hard and tinkling. "Oh, I can't lose myself in the crowd here, if that's what's troubling you."

85

He went into the drugstore and left her standing outside, watching the sleepy little street, free for a moment from the oppression of his presence.

But still a prisoner of the black chaos of her own thoughts, in which one phrase beat itself over and over . . . *and the dead body of the child was subsequently discovered . . .*

She shivered and tried desperately to fathom the connection between the child in the swamp and the man lying at her feet in the Steinmark library and the man crouching by the French doors outside. And between all these and Joanna Starr and that fifty thousand dollars in denominations of five hundred dollars.

One of those five hundred dollar bills was gone, swift messenger to the police, blazing the trail she had left behind her. The balance of that great fistful had been in her purse when they had left the hotel. Now it was in the pocket of Paul Saniel. He had made her give it to him, for if she had not he would have taken it by force.

"For safekeeping," he had said, and his face was twisted and bitter and ugly. "And for future reference—perhaps."

But he hadn't questioned her about it.

Just as she hadn't questioned him about that jagged three-cornered tear on the pocket of his coat, the one for which the New York Police Department held the patch.

She hadn't questioned him, but that night, last night, she had tugged and pulled a heavy dresser in front of the door which led from her bedroom. And now she was always beside him. Not in front.

And they walked in mutual mistrust and nameless fear and suspicion.

Together they had performed the simple duties of the cabin, preparing breakfast and lunch, washing the dishes and making beds. Wordless but watching—each one the other.

She had stood beside him while he filed numbers off the Chevrolet coupé. She had handed him tools like some willing helper, and once while he was bending over she had seen a heavy wrench in the toolbox. Then he had straightened quickly and caught her eyes and read the thoughts behind them, and he had locked the toolbox.

She had been beside him on that last ride as he searched for some high cliff and remote ravine where a car, once it had a slight push, would conveniently smash itself to pieces. He had made no explanation of the destruction, for none was necessary.

Only now that act of vandalism—and the story that was in the paper the night before—put them in the same category. WANTED BY THE POLICE. The sort of thing you saw on placards on the walls of rural post offices. With photographs, front and side view. But there were no photographs of her, she remembered with satisfaction. The old road company, of course, had photographs of Helen Varney, but heavily disguised in character parts.

She was brought up with a sudden start by a hasty hand on her arm and a low voice, a bit breathless. "Get going! Quick." And he half pulled her along as he walked rapidly down the tiny street and struck off into the path that led to the woods. There was a big bundle of newspapers under his arm. Nothing else.

"Wait," she protested, hanging back. "You forgot. We need coffee at the grocery and—"

"Never mind about coffee." And he almost jerked her along the trail.

Both of them were breathless when they reached the crest of the first rise and dropped down behind it into a little valley. Only then did he slacken pace, but he made no explanation.

But when they got back to the cabin and the kerosene lamp threw its feeble light on the bundle of papers he had brought, she understood. There was his picture. Two columns wide. Right there on the front page. "Paul Saniel, whose disappearance police are linking with the Steinmark murder case."

An excellent likeness, full face. Anyone who took the trouble—the clerk in the drugstore, a chance village loafer—could recognize the original of the picture in spite of a three days' growth of dark stubble.

She looked at the photograph beside it. A girl, this one, with the same dark hair curling up from a low forehead, the same deep-set, dark eyes ". . . sought by the police in the murder of Hugo . . ."

It was Joanna Starr—the real Joanna, not the one standing here in the half-light of a coal oil lamp in a lonely cabin in the woods. ". . . identified as Joanna Starr of the West Eighty-seventh Street address, but not the Joanna Starr who was at the Steinmark house when . . ."

Suddenly she felt him very close to her. She whirled quickly and drew back. It was there again, that black, unleashed fury. Only now there were no restraints. There was no music and movement of other people. No crowded city about them, only the empty silence of trees and hills.

His eyes were blazing with a fierce, passionate anger. It was as if the hours of watching and waiting had at last completed their subtle erosion, and emotion long restrained and damned up burst forth in savage frenzy.

"Where is she? *Where is she?*"

"I . . . I don't know."

"You're lying."

He moved toward her. She backed away and grabbed a chair to thrust between them. He jerked it from her; sent it skidding across the floor, crashing against the footboards.

"Tell me where she is." He was shouting now. "What have you done with her? If you've killed her, I'll—" He grabbed hold of her.

"I haven't done anything to her. I don't know where—"

"You're lying. You're a lying, murdering bitch!"

She screamed; fought off the hands that encircled her neck; tore at the steel bands closing in on her throat, at the brutal thumbs gouging into her windpipe . . . shutting off air.

For a moment she saw eyes blazing with fury, and white lips . . . felt his breath in hot spasms . . . then no more, for the fierce pounding in her temples . . . something inside her head pounding to get out . . . pounding . . . something tearing at her lungs . . . prisms of light zigzagging through blackness . . .

She didn't open her eyes right away.

She didn't move. She just lay there and let the soft blackness lap around her like soothing waves. Her head felt heavy and damp; and there was a funny sound, a little rasping sound.

As the mists clogging brain and consciousness receded she realized that she herself was making the little rasping sound, drawing breath in through her raw throat. But still she did not stir nor open her eyes. It was enough just to lie there and feel the blessed air filling her lungs. Not to struggle. Not to fight off fierce hands.

But there were hands now, on her forehead, chafing her wrists. Not fierce hands. Trembling hands!

Consciousness returned in a full, steady tide, and she felt every nerve stiffen within her. But she did not move. He was bending over her. She could feel his muscles quivering and hear his breath coming quickly.

She opened her eyes. For one swift moment she caught the look in his. Then hurriedly the blinds were lowered and once more the blank façade was in place.

"Would you like a drink of water?" he asked, and his voice was as flat and colorless as when he had said, "Would you like a liqueur . . . Shall we dance?"

12

Late moonlight seeped through the dark branches, and the soft wind that precedes the dawn ruffled the treetops. Joanna Starr leaned against the window casing and stared out into the silvery night.

She was in the bedroom of the cabin. The door to the main room was closed, the heavy dresser in front of it.

She gripped the window casing, seeking something hard and resistant to bring to her a sense of reality, something firm in a chaos of tumultuous emotions.

Hours had passed since he had helped her into her room, lit the lamp, even left the papers for her. Fantastic! And a bit silly, those gestures of restrained solicitude for someone he had just attempted to strangle.

She tried to sort out her own emotions. Fear and terror and bewilderment and doubt and uncertainty and haunting, gnawing questions. New questions now to add their burden to the old ones.

She felt again those trembling hands, saw again that brief look that she had caught in his eyes. She stared out into the moonlight and her hands went up to her face in an instinctive gesture of self-confession. And protest!

He belonged to another woman. And he and that other woman were inextricably involved in all the dark horror of kidnaping and murder.

She jerked the curtain down to shut out the moonlight and crossed to the dresser and lit the lamp. She carried it to a table by the bed and spread the newspapers out once again and reread a long column.

> Police are said to be working on the theory that the real Joanna Starr was a member of a kidnap gang, and that she ratted and decided through an intermediary, Hugo Steinmark, to turn the Newberger ransom money back to Newberger. It is believed she had a date with Steinmark for this purpose but that before she could keep it her betrayal was discovered by another member of the gang, probably a woman. The theory is that this other woman killed the real Joanna Starr and . . .

That was it! . . . *killed the real Joanna Starr.* He believed it. That was why fury and anger had sent him clutching savagely at her throat. Then why hadn't he gone ahead with the job? It didn't make sense.

She read on.

> The theory is that this second woman killed the real Joanna Starr and took her name and place and then killed Steinmark. It is believed that Steinmark was expecting the ransom money Thursday night and intended to turn it over to Newberger the next morning. Instead he got a bullet. Police searching for the body of the real Joanna Starr . . .

She put the paper down. She must think. She must solve the riddle of the relationship between Joanna Starr and Paul Saniel. They were the cornerstone, the key to the whole horrible, crazy puzzle.

Her eyes that had been staring vacantly in front of her in desperate concentration were suddenly arrested. There on the other side of the room, on the floor, where the dresser had stood . . . Just a scrap of paper, but there was a name in big, bold handwriting that she could read even at a distance.

She rose from the bed and tiptoed softly across the rough pine boards of the cabin, stooped and retrieved the scrap of paper. She took it back to the light. A letter. Or rather part of a letter. The lower half of a single sheet of heavy white note paper.

She read slowly the few lines that were sprawled across the half page. She read through to the signature at the bottom. And then for a long moment she just stared at it, letting the implication of those sprawling words take shape, sink in.

She was back at the dresser, hunting through the drawers. But they were empty of all save a few innocuous odds and ends. Nervous hands pawed over other odds and ends on a bookshelf under the window, behind the cretonne curtain' that formed an impromptu closet, even under the one rough Indian rug. But it wasn't there, anywhere, that other half of the letter.

Finally she gave it up, sat down on the bed and reread the torn scrap.

"... and so, my darling Jo, I'll kill you. If you ever rat on me, my love will turn to pure poison and I'll come three thousand miles to cut your throat.—Paul."

She put down the letter and her eyes sought the newspaper she had been reading.

... that the real Joanna Starr was a member of a kidnap gang and that she ratted ...

The real Joanna *had ratted!*

Suddenly it was clear. Horribly clear. The Newberger child had been kidnaped and murdered and fifty thousand dollars ransom money collected. And the real Joanna had known it, had even had the fifty thousand dollars. And then she had told Hugo Steinmark.

But why Steinmark? What was he to her? No, no, that was all right. There was a logical link there. Steinmark, was Trudi Hess's husband. And Trudi Hess had been in Hollywood with Paul Saniel. And Paul Saniel was bound up with the real Joanna. It all hitched up, one person to another.

And so she had told Steinmark and he had promised to turn the money back to Newberger for her.

... I'll come three thousand miles to cut ...

Well, he had come—to kill her. But when he got there she had escaped him, left in her place another Joanna. So he had followed the other Joanna. Followed her to the Steinmark house that Thursday night, hidden in the bushes beside the window. He was a thief, a kidnaper, a murderer.

The sense of danger which had encompassed her heightened to imminent peril, spread itself to include the real Joanna. Both of them, the real as well as the false. She must get out, get away, find the real Joanna. Warn her. Or didn't she need warning? Anyway, snatch back the safe nonentity of Helen Varney, an out-of-work actress waiting on table. No one could hold her to the bargain now.

Escape! Escape from *him!*

And then mingled with fear was another emotion, equally strong, equally compelling, another inner voice speaking crazy counsel. She started up from the bed and was halfway across the room to the door before she caught herself and staggered back.

She turned out the light and for a long moment sat there in the stillness of the night, her icy hands clutching her throat where hours before his hands had been fastened in a brutal grip.

Then, moving quickly but very quietly, she put on her shoes and reached for her hat on the bookshelf beneath the window. She had not undressed, so she was ready now. Stealthily from the top drawer of the dresser she took her handbag, and felt in the darkness for the change purse. A few bills, some miscellaneous silver. But enough.

She lit a match and looked at her watch. Three-thirty. Once out of the cabin and onto the road it would take her about three quarters of an hour to get to the village. She prayed that there would be a milk train to the city and that it would stop.

She tiptoed to the dresser, where there were scissors. Manicure scissors. Delicate and foolish. She looked at them doubtfully, wondered if they would be equal to their task. She longed for a pair of stout shears.

She crossed softly to the window and raised the shade and lifted the scissors to cut—

To cut the screen. But there was no screen. There had been last night and the night before. She was sure of that, because she had looked at the window and speculated. There had been a screen then. Now there was only a gaping, unobstructed opening.

Had it been that way only half an hour before, when she had stared out into the moonlight? Had she been too shattered and be-wildered by emotion to notice that it was not there? Or had it been removed since then?

She laid the silly scissors on the shelf and slipped through the window into the waning night.

13

At eight o'clock in the morning, Unit 7 of Jason Restaurants on Sixth Avenue was still sleepy and uncrowded. Most people had their breakfasts at home. The rush didn't really begin until eleven, and only half the staff was on duty.

At least that was the way it seemed to Joanna Starr, sitting with a cup of coffee and a roll at the back near the door into the kitchen. There weren't many waitresses about. Her eyes flashed in turn on each new one that she spied, gave her a quick glance, then roved around the room to the next one.

Perhaps it would have been better to have gone to the Brooklyn rooming house. Perhaps she came on for the noon hour rush. Would she dare ask outright for Helen Varney? Better not. Only attract attention. Better just sit and dawdle over coffee.

She motioned to a waitress, a fresh, pretty blond girl.

"More coffee, please."

"Yes'm." The waitress picked up her cup, refilled it at the big, steaming coffee urn and brought it back.

"Hot, isn't it?" she said pleasantly as she set the cup down.

Joanna Starr forced herself to smile. "You mean the coffee or the weather?"

"Both." The waitress lingered at the table after making sure with a swift glance that there were no customers at her other tables. "Weather like this you'd almost rather drink iced tea for breakfast."

She was disposed to talk, and on second thought Joanna Starr encouraged her. "Not much of a rush on now, is there?"

"Just wait until lunchtime. It's terrible then. It'll be worse to-day. We're shorthanded."

"Maybe I could get a job then."

"Say now, there's something to that if you're looking for one. If the employment office don't get another girl over here by noon we're going to have to do some doubling up. One of our girls left yesterday. Say"—the waitress leaned over confidentially, sharing an excitement—"I guess you read about the girl that left yesterday."

"What about her?" Joanna Starr felt an uneasy premonition.

"You saw that picture that was in yesterday of Joanna Starr, that girl that's wanted in the Steinmark murder case? Well, that picture wasn't of Joanna Starr at all. It was a picture of a girl working here. A girl named Helen Varney."

Joanna Starr laid her spoon down quietly to keep it born clattering on the porcelain tabletop, forced herself to speak casually. "Well . . . well, what do you know!"

"Her picture was in the paper yesterday morning and she never showed up for work and she hasn't been back since. I understand the manager went to the police and— Sorry, got a customer."

She stared unseeing in front of her. Why hadn't she foreseen this? She'd been stupid. She should have gone immediately to the Brooklyn rooming house. She picked up her bag, waited impatiently for her check.

"With you in just a minute." The pretty blond girl stopped hurriedly as she brushed by the table. There was a newspaper in her hand, left by a departing customer. "See, here's some more about that girl I was telling you about." She laid a morning paper on the table and hurried through the door to the kitchen.

Joanna Starr's eyes fell on the headlines streaming across the page and the story beneath it.

> . . . further complicated by the fact that the police immediately on hearing the story of the Jason Restaurant manager went to the rooming house of the girl, Helen Varney. The landlady said that she had left hurriedly that morning without leaving any

address. The photograph in question has been identified both as Joanna Starr and as Helen Varney. In
other words, the police are now searching for one
girl with two names and for a second girl with no
name, although the second one, it has been pointed
out, assumed the name of Joanna Starr for a brief
period before the Steinmark murder. Confusion in
the . . .

When her check came she went forward to the cashier's desk,
her mind still in a dazed struggle with the new turn of events. She
pushed check and money through the grille, waited for change, listened unconsciously with half her brain to the conversation of the
cashier and a dawdling waitress.

". . . see, finding Joanna Starr alive and working here under the
name of Helen Varney sort of knocks into a cocked hat that theory
that the police had about her being murdered."

"Say, but have you seen the *Gazette?* There's a hot story in
there. It seems that this Paul Saniel and Trudi Hess . . ." The cashier's voice lowered.

She picked up her change and went out into the early morning
sunshine. She looked around for a newsstand, bought a *Gazette.* She
couldn't read standing up on the sidewalk, but there was a little park
there to her right. She could see trees a block away. Madison Square.

She found a bench among the early morning idlers, spread the
paper across her knees.

There was his photograph again on the front page, but a different one this time. And across the corner there was a scrawl of
writing, an intimate, affectionate inscription.

There was a picture of Trudi Hess, of course, beside his. She
was wearing the long, white-cowled gown and an Eleonora Duse
expression and she looked very tragic. Beneath the two pictures
was a story with a Hollywood date line.

Are Trudi Hess, international film star; Paul Saniel,
her director; and Hugo Steinmark, murdered theatrical

producer of New York, the three angles of a trans-
continental love triangle?

This is the question which police in New York
and Hollywood are trying to answer in an effort to
find the murderer of Steinmark. Trudi Hess now
claims the slain Steinmark as her husband, and has
emphatically denied that she and her director are
anything more than "just good friends," but Hollywood hot spots are lifting skeptical eyebrows. It is
rumored that . . .

That was the way the whole story read. It is rumored . . . There
were said to be . . . The alleged affair between the star and her
director . . . Insinuation, innuendo, backstairs gossip, cunning
suggestion, caustic comment. Whispers and hints and malice and
acid. Nothing you could pin down, put your finger on. Every phrase
within the legal limits imposed by the statutes dealing with libel.

And yet there wasn't a doubt about what the unknown author
meant—that Trudi Hess and Paul Saniel were lovers, and that Hugo
Steinmark was the only obstacle to the legalization of a relationship
that for months had been the talk of Hollywood.

She put down the paper. Paul Saniel had called Joanna Starr
his "darling." Yet his affair with Trudi Hess had been the talk of
Hollywood. New unanswerable questions crowded into her brain,
hammering at her nerves.

And it was all so foolish now, so futile. She was through with
them all. Through with Joanna Starr and Paul Saniel and Hugo
Steinmark and all of them. She was a nobody now, a nonentity
again, one of ten million. No need now to fear or worry, to walk
furtively or hide. She was free of all the dark horror.

She rose wearily from the park bench. With the easing of emotional tension there came the realization that she was tired, that
she had not slept for more than twenty-four hours and that tonight
she would lay her head again on some hot rooming house pillow
beneath some baking brownstone roof.

She walked slowly, aimlessly, along the tree-shaded paths of
the park, emerged into the hot sun of the sidewalk, started to step
from the curb.

"Wait until the light changes."

She felt a hand on her arm holding her back. Heard a voice. She turned, startled.

It was a man. Middle-aged, with graying temples. Hat pulled down over the eyes. A small graying mustache. But there was something queer about him. Then suddenly she knew.

It was Paul Saniel. And he was smiling.

14

It was like an unnerving blow. Not one that shot tense caution through veins, that stiffened muscles to watchful alertness, but one that left nerves and muscles quivering and helpless.

Smiling! From eyes that were deep-ringed with strain and weariness but quiet with a sense of almost shattering relief—as if some black burden too great to be borne had suddenly been lifted, leaving him weak and frazzled but with a strange peace.

She felt herself swaying. The street seemed to swim about her and a wave of heat rise up from the pavement. She felt his steadying hand on her arm, strong but without that old threatening menace.

"Taxi," he called, and she was gently propelled into a seat just as her knees gave way beneath her. She felt herself trembling, felt weak tears rising in her throat. And didn't care.

He gave a brief order to the driver and they moved into the northbound stream of traffic. He didn't talk, and she was glad of that. He only kept that steadying hand on her arm and, inexplicably, she was glad of that too.

Slowly the wave of heat receded and the swimming blur that was before her eyes dissolved into Fifth Avenue.

Presently he spoke. "Have you had anything to eat?"

Simple, workaday words. Anticlimax words, but solid and good in their simplicity. She nodded.

They drove a long time, up the Avenue until they left behind its swank, though dreary tenements, over a bridge, into a maze of small apartment houses.

They got out and he paid off the driver and they walked along a street for several blocks. He was hunting for something. She didn't know what. She was still too dazed to care. She was still only an automaton responding to the touch of his hand on her arm.

They turned in at a real estate office and there was talk of a furnished apartment.

"For my—niece and myself," she heard him say.

"My niece." That was she. "We've just come on from Chicago."

The apartment was a few blocks away. On the third floor of a walk-up. Three rooms with nondescript furniture. He talked some more to the man who had come with them, and then pulled out money and signed something. Signed J. H. Pollock. And the man left.

The door closed behind him and they were alone. He opened the windows and drew a chair up to one of them and she sat down. He drew up another chair opposite her and seated himself.

"I think, my dear," he said quietly, "it's time you and I had a little talk." And he smiled again, the kind of smile one gives to a frightened child to drive away its fears.

He offered her a cigarette, took one himself. With the relaxation that comes with the initial inhale, she spoke for the first time.

"How did you find me?"

"I never lost you. I caught the hind end of the milk train that had you on the front end."

"Then it was deliberate? I mean the screen? You took it out, let me go?"

He nodded.

"Why?"

"I'd tried one method and it didn't work. So I tried another. I wanted to see whether, if I let you 'escape,' you'd lead me to Joanna Starr."

Joanna Starr. The name suddenly stiffened something within her.

He went on in the same patient voice. "Why didn't you tell me she was safe? That you hadn't made away with her?"

She made no answer.

"Don't you see? Don't you understand? I didn't know whether she was dead or alive. If she were alive you were the only one who could lead me to her. You were the only link I had with her. So I hung on to you desperately.

"But I was afraid of making a false move and gumming the whole works, so I played a waiting game. I thought it might wear you down. That you'd give in at last and tell me where she was. And then when you didn't it began to wear me down. I began to think that perhaps she was dead. And that you killed her. Until—"

He broke off and the eyes that had been looking so frankly into hers dropped. "I don't like to think of it. I'd kept it in for so long that it suddenly boiled over. Seeing her picture there in the paper. I suppose that's what did it. I went mad, berserk. I—I almost killed you."

He rose and took a swift turn up and down the little room as if he would work off the oppressive, shameful memory of that last night in the cabin.

"But now, of course," he resumed presently, "everything is different. I feel as if I'd come through a horrible nightmare. It's still dark, but there's light ahead. It isn't all plain sailing yet. But at least now I know. . . And I'm a bit giddy with relief."

He looked it. He acted it. There was a buoyancy about him in spite of the heavy lines of fatigue in his face. He knew that his Joanna was alive. He looked as if he wanted to shout and sing.

Had she been wrong about him all along? Had it been necessary to protect the real Joanna from him? Had it been he who had brought that look of hunted fear into the other girl's eyes—this man standing now before her, weak and undone almost with the knowledge that somewhere in the world, in the city, his "darling" was alive and he had only to find her?

"And so that's why we've got to have a little talk. You and I." He flung himself down again in the chair, leaned toward her. "We've got to find Jo. And we've got to clear you."

The hand holding her cigarette paused suddenly in mid-air, then lowered slowly. *And we've got to clear you.* That other part of the picture momentarily pushed into the background of her consciousness, leaped into clear outline again.

"Because you know, my dear," he was saying, "you didn't kill Hugo Steinmark."

The cold caution that had held her in its grip for three days suddenly returned, lapped again at the fringes of her emotion. All the things she had forgotten began crowding back into her consciousness, bringing with them all the old implications of menace and fear.

No, not all of them. Not for the real Joanna. Let him find the real Joanna himself. She'd been silly, protecting when no protection was necessary. It was herself she had to protect now.

From the man who had been that night at the Steinmark house, who had crouched in the bushes by the French door, who even now with an assumption of engaging honesty was fashioning a cunning pitfall to trap her.

Or was he?

Her mind was like a drawer that had been turned upside down, its contents scattered, disorganized, strewn about in a crazy helter-skelter out of which she could salvage no order or coherence.

"So tell me," she heard him saying persuasively. "Tell me all about it. Start from the beginning."

She raised her eyes to meet his and the retort burst from her. "Hunt up your Joanna and ask her."

15

Eth Hawley of Upper Riverton, New York, collected homely items for the *Upper Riverton Weekly Clarion* and cherished an ambition to be a New York police reporter. The New York morning paper which he snatched from the early morning mail train seemed to suggest a compromise.

Helen Varney . . . involved in the notorious Steinmark case. Missing? . . . Murdered? . . . Helen Varney! But that was Miss Sophy Pratt's niece that had run away two years back with a traveling road company.

Eth made the distance from the depot to Miss Sophy's cottage in nothing fiat. He was panting and he had lost his hat but not his head.

"Miss Sophy—quick—*pictures!*" He sank into one of the front porch chairs.

Miss Sophy laid down the *Sunday School Times* and looked over her glasses. "*What* pictures?"

"Helen, your niece. Helen Varney. She— Look!" He waved the papers before her.

"Eth Hawley, what are you talking about? Are you crazy!"

"There, see. Read about Helen." He pointed to a headline. POLICE CONSIDER MURDER THEORY IN DISAPPEARANCE OF JOANNA STARR–HELEN VARNEY.

Miss Sophy's eyes popped. She snatched the paper from him and devoured the first column. She was shocked! And triumphant.

"I knew it," she affirmed righteously. "I always knew it. No good end for—"

"But, Miss Sophy, pictures," Eth protested. "I've got to have 'em quick. If I can get 'em off on the down train, the New York papers'll eat 'em up. Maybe I'd even get a job, but I haven't got any time to lose."

Miss Sophy looked exasperated. "Eth Hawley, you are crazy. Here my only niece is murdered and you sit there and talk about pictures. What pictures?"

"Hers. Don't you see? They can't find her, but if they had a picture of her, a photograph, maybe they could. Maybe she ain't murdered at all. Maybe she's been kidnaped and held by a gang. Maybe she's hiding out. Maybe . . ."

He finally convinced her that it was her duty as a citizen to aid the police. Eth knew her well enough to realize that emotional appeals to affection were futile. But duty was one of the cornerstones of Miss Sophy's life.

She produced pictures—all that she had.

Eth looked at them and his face fell. Then he looked at his watch. He had just fifteen minutes. He snatched up the pictures and ran.

"I see by the papers," said Paul Saniel as he propped his feet comfortably on the window sill and scanned the *World-Telegram*, "I see by the papers that your stomach is adorable."

Joanna Starr didn't even gasp or start or flare with indignation. She was beyond the lesser emotions. Beyond trying to find the key to this man who sat opposite her now reading the evening papers. This fellow who had taken the place of Paul Saniel, this fellow who laughed and was gay. No, giddy. That was his own term. Like someone who emerges from a long dark tunnel, giddy and blinking with the sudden light.

She had flung her retort at him. *Hunt up your Joanna and ask her*. And not all his persuasiveness could worm its way past the barrier she had put up. Their "little talk" had foundered on that one sentence.

"All right," he had said, "if that's the way you want it, that's the way it shall be."

But there was no more silent, watchful distrust. Speech bubbled forth in a spate of talk that flowed free and unhindered. He had even given her a ten dollar bill and sent her to the corner grocery store for supplies, and when she had returned he was asleep on the couch.

"I could have run away," she pointed out to him.

"I know, but I had to risk that. I can't go on playing jailer all my life. And anyway"—he shrugged his shoulder—"it doesn't seem to do much good."

She could have run away. But she hadn't. She had come back. To herself she tried to rationalize that illogical return, tried not to admit it, tried to push back into the subconscious the crazy folly of her own emotions.

"You were snoring," she had accused him.

He grinned. "That's because I have a clear conscience. Or maybe it's the artist in me. I'm just carried away by the role of your aged uncle. I remember once when I was playing in a picture at . . ."

He had been an actor of sorts, before he became a director, and he launched into reminiscences of days on the set. He even told her how he had prepared himself for his aged uncle role that night in the cabin while he waited for her to "escape."

She had cooked a meal while he had gone out for the evening papers, and they had eaten it, and now he was stretched out comfortably scanning the news.

"I repeat, my dear—your stomach is adorable. Or perhaps I should say was adorable. At six months anyway." And he tossed over the paper he had been reading.

The baby was fat, with dimples peeking out of chubby knees and elbows; and the stomach was adorable, with creases of soft baby flesh running crossways and disappearing into the white fur.

The pose was one beloved of small town photographers when confronted with an infant. Naked on a bear rug struggling valiantly to put the left toe under the right tooth.

It occupied the central position on the front page, flanked on one side by a grinning six-year-old with two front teeth missing and on the other side by a nice old lady with glasses and a shawl and wrinkles.

Only known photographs of the girl whose name, Helen Varney, was assumed by Joanna Starr, involved in the Steinmark murder mystery. Are they photographs of the "lady in lilac" whose fingerprints were found on the gun that killed Steinmark and for whom the police have been searching for almost a week? (Story on page 3)

The paper crackled as she whipped the front page under and turned to page three. The story was from Upper Riverton with a by-line that read *Ethan W. Hawley.*

Further complications were injected into the already complicated Steinmark murder case with the claim here today by Miss Sophy Pratt that Helen Varney, whose name has figured prominently in the mystery, is her niece who ran away from home two years ago to join a traveling theatrical company and has not been heard from since.

Miss Pratt states emphatically that the picture identified by a photographer and apartment house attendants as Joanna Starr, and by employees at the Sixth Avenue Jason Restaurant as a waitress named Helen Varney, is not her niece, Helen Varney. It is her belief that . . .

She read to the end of the column.

"Was she pretty awful?" he said.

"Who?"

"Aunt Sophy. I can feel for you. Of course I had parents, but when I decided to go on the stage they cast me off. I had to run away from home and change my name, too. Only I just made one up. I didn't swipe someone's else like you. You should have told me about it, though. We could have had such fun comparing notes."

"Aren't you assuming a lot?"

"How so?"

"That I'm this—this Helen Varney."

"Well, aren't you?"

"No." The lie rolled off glibly.

"And you're not Joanna Starr?"

"No."

His brows knitted into a frown of deep thought. Then suddenly the lightning of a brilliant idea struck him. "I know! You're the missing Charlie Ross!"

"Don't be a fool."

"Don't get mad. I was only trying to keep you company."

"Meaning I'm a fool?"

"Right. Otherwise you'd break down and tell me all."

She considered this warily. "Suppose," she said slowly, "you start it."

"Start what?"

"Telling all."

"Me?" He was indignant with mock surprise. "I have nothing to tell. My life is an open book."

"With the usual pages glued together."

"For instance?"

"Well, the ones on which the name of Joanna Starr is written."

"She seems to trouble you. Is it your conscience hurting because you stole her name and telegraph address?"

"I'm sorry about the telegram. I mean opening it."

"Why strain at gnats after you've swallowed a whole herd of camels?"

"But of course," she said, and her voice took on a new iciness, "of course you don't mind having your personal affairs spread about."

"I don't know what you mean, but I have a suspicion that it's unpleasant. What's bearing down on your chest?"

"Nothing. It doesn't bother me."

"What's 'it' that isn't bothering you? Or since 'it' isn't bothering you, maybe I better not bother 'it.' Whatever 'it' is."

"Yes, perhaps that's much the best plan. Let sleeping dogs lie. You doubtless prefer that, but the police and the newspapers hardly seem to be in an accommodating mood."

For a moment he looked bewildered. Then slow realization came. He grinned, then grew serious. Or was it mock-serious?

"You are referring, I take it, to the great love affair served up from Hollywood in the *Gazette?*"

She nodded.

"Ah, well, that's the price of fame. Even our most sacred emotions sullied."

She rose abruptly.

"What's the matter? Where are you going?"

"To the kitchen to get a drink of water. It's quite useless to talk to a fool."

"O. K. We're even now. I called you a fool and you called me one. Let's start all over again from scratch."

He followed her into the kitchen and sat on the edge of the table while she gathered ice cubes from the frigidaire.

"Jo, darling!"

No answer.

"Helen, love!"

Silence.

"I'll have to make up a name then. How about 'Dimples'? Or don't you have 'em anymore? Or maybe 'Cuddles'? Or I know— 'Pinkey.' Listen, Pinkey, get out some more ice, and I'll squeeze oranges and we'll—"

Suddenly she whirled on him. "Stop it!"

"What am I doing?"

"Talking. Talking around and around in circles, just as if . . . as if . . ."

"As if what?"

"As if we weren't *us*. Two people bound up with murder, wanted by the police. You going around disguised. Me using a name that isn't my own. Hiding here in this apartment. What's going to be the end of it? What are we going to do next? Or what are *you* going to do?"

He grew sober as she flung the question at him. "I've already told you. First, find Jo."

He gave a hasty glance at his wrist watch. "And perhaps I had better get busy about it right now." He turned and started from the room.

"Where are you going?"

He paused. "I'm going to smoke out Joanna-Helen-Varney-Starr. I'll be late getting back." As he opened the door his face broke into a grin again.

"Don't wait up for me—*Pinkey*," he called over his shoulder.

But she did. In the bedroom, lying tense and wakeful, listening for the sound of a key in the lock, wondering, turning things over slowly in her mind.

But no longer seeking for answers she couldn't find. She was through with that. Resolution was beginning to gather, congeal, take shape. Not very definite shape, to be sure, but something more positive than the empty gropings of the last days.

It was after eleven when he got back. She could hear him moving about, taking off his shoes, creaking the couch as he settled down for the night. And then presently she could hear deep, even breathing.

She opened the door a crack, waited. Then she crept into the living room. In the faint light that came from the street lamps she could see that he was asleep and his clothes were scattered about the room. His trousers in one chair, his coat hanging over a table near the window.

She picked it up, smoothed out the wrinkles. Her hand caught on the three-cornered tear over the pocket. She wondered again about the swatch of brown tweed the police had found outside the Steinmark window. As she went to hang the coat over the back of a chair, something fell out with a soft thud.

It was a key. A piece of paper slipped out with it. She replaced the key; held the piece of paper in her hands for a few moments, thoughtful. Then she crept back into the bedroom with it and turned on the shaded bed light.

A receipt, from the upper Bronx office of the *New York Times*, for a classified advertisement. She looked at the date. Today. That's what he had gone out for . . . *to smoke out Joanna-Helen-Varney-Starr.*

Very early the next morning before he was awake she crept out of her room into the living room. He was still sleeping soundly. She tiptoed to the chair beside his couch and picked up the clock and switched off the alarm. Then, just as quietly, she tiptoed out of the apartment and closed the door behind her.

She had on her hat and she carried her bag, and at the news-stand she bought a copy of the *New York Times* and turned to the classified advertising section.

16

The maid at the home of Charles W. Newberger was puzzled by the girl who had just rang the front doorbell.

"Mr. Newberger did not say anything about a nurse."

"But I have it right here—the ad. See." And the girl thrust forward a paper. The *New York Times* folded to the Help Wanted, Female section.

> NURSE in early twenties for small boy in $50,000
> home. Experience unnecessary. But *absolute securi-*
> *ty* offered to right party.— Newberger.

"This is the right place, isn't it?" the girl insisted as she pointed to the address that followed "Newberger."

"Yes, but there's no small boy here—now." A look of puzzled distress crossed the maid's face. "Perhaps you had better wait and speak to Mr. Newberger."

She led the way through a dimly lighted hall to a room at the left looking out onto the street. "Mr. Newberger isn't up yet. It's very early."

"I'll wait," the girl said, and glanced at her watch. Eight o'clock. She was the first one there. That was as it should be. She settled herself in an easy chair and waited, and watched through the window that gave onto the street.

Presently there was another girl, and another and another, each one carrying the *New York Times* want ad section. They seated themselves stiffly and surveyed the room in hostile silence, seeing in one another competitors in the heartbreaking search for jobs.

Only the girl by the window seemed indifferent to her potential rivals. She was watching the steps that led up to the house.

Suddenly her pulse quickened. There . . . mounting the steps . . . ringing the bell . . . standing at last in the doorway that led into the crowded reception room from the hall.

"But I must see Mr. Newberger," the girl was protesting to the maid, and there was a terrible urgency in her voice.

"I know," the maid said complacently, for by this time she had become used to this strange influx of applicants. "Just wait in here with the others."

"Others?" She cast a swift, questioning glance at the room crowded with girls. "But there aren't any others. I'm the one. I'm the one he wants."

But the maid was adamant. She had already had the *New York Times* thrust at her half a dozen times. She gave the girl a slight push into the room and closed the door behind her.

For a moment the girl just stood there, and the hands that held the paper quivered. She was pale and distrait and her clothes were rumpled as if she had slept in them, and her heavy dark hair was pulled back into a careless knot as if no feminine reinforcements of looking glass and powder and pressing iron had been available to her toilette. To the casual glance a girl who bore only the slightest resemblance to a carefully posed studio portrait, enhanced by all the clever tricks of lighting and retouching.

But it was the eyes that looked out from dark shadows that spoke the full measure of despair. Hunted eyes, harboring in their depths doubt and fear. They traveled now about the room, sometimes slowly, sometimes in nervous jerks. And then suddenly they were caught up short, and she stifled a little gasp.

Joanna Starr and Helen Varney looked at each other across the width of the room. Joanna Starr sitting by the window. Helen Varney standing by the door. Or was it the other way around? The real Joanna by the door and the real Helen by the window?

There was no seat vacant; but there were wide arms to the chair by the window, and the girl sitting there rose and gave an almost imperceptible backward jerk of her head. The girl by the door hesitated. Then she walked slowly across the room and took the proffered chair. The other girl sat on one of the heavy, upholstered arms.

For a moment neither one of them said anything. Both were striving to still a clamant, inner trembling.

Then the girl in the seat half whispered to the girl on the arm, "I didn't mean to let you in for . . . for . . ." She groped for words.

"Yes, I know. But never mind about that now."

She was cut short by the opening of the door leading into the hall and a man's voice. He was standing there surveying with weary, tormented eyes the room full of girls.

"There's been some mistake, young women," he was saying. "I inserted no ad in the *Times* for a nurse."

Joanna Starr felt the sudden pull of the other girl's hand on her knee as she extricated herself from the deep chair seat and started across the room toward the man in the doorway.

"But, Mr. Newberger!"

"I'm sorry. You'll have to take your turn with the others."

"But . . . but I . . ."

He silenced her with a gesture. "There has been some mistake," he repeated. "Something queer. I've telephoned my lawyer and asked him to come up here. I must ask you to wait until he arrives so that he can talk to each one of you individually."

There were murmurs of protest and resentment.

"I know. I'm sorry. Terribly sorry. I'll reimburse all of you for transportation wasted on a wild goose chase. The maid will bring in coffee and sandwiches for those who haven't had any breakfast, but you must— I will forcibly detain anyone who tries to leave before my lawyer has had a chance to see her." He burst out with the last like a man under some fierce compulsion that leaps over barriers of mere legality.

There were more murmurs, but not so much protest, as they fell to the coffee and sandwiches that a maid brought in. Only the two girls by the window did not join in.

"Don't talk now," the one on the arm was saying. "Wait until we've each seen the lawyer and then we'll meet outside."

"But I must see Mr. Newberger. That's what I should have done in the first place—in the very beginning."

"All right, all right. Later. But just for the present—"

"I don't believe him. It isn't a mistake. It was a message to me. That about the small boy and the $50,000 and the nurse 'in her early twenties.' And security. '*Absolute security.*' Did you see that? Did you see how it was underlined? That meant he'd protect me. And now he's trying to back out."

"Hush. Not now, I tell you. Not here." She shut off the rising shrillness of the other girl and glanced nervously around to see if anyone had overheard. "We'll talk it all over when we get out of here. We'll—"

And now it was she in turn who was cut off short by the other girl. The real Joanna had shrunk back, huddling down, seeking the slight protection offered by the girl on the arm. Her knuckles were white where she clutched the chair.

"Look—there—he—"

The girl who had taken the name of Joanna Starr looked out of the window. And was puzzled.

A taxicab had drawn up in front of the house and a man was getting out, paying off the driver, walking up the steps to the New-berger house.

The cab from which he had emerged drove off and then she saw something which it had obstructed. Another man across the street. Leaning against a lamppost, smoking a cigarette, looking for all the world like a casual loafer killing time. Paul Saniel!

She felt her muscles stiffen. So he'd wakened. Late because she had turned off the alarm. He had grabbed his clothes and rushed off to the Newberger house, and now he was waiting.

For the real Joanna!

Suddenly all her emotions and reasoning underwent another of those shattering reversals, tipped over again into helter-skelter chaos. When she had found the ad in the *Times* she had seen through his plan, had formed a plan of her own. A bold plan that would carry her right into enemy territory, but new courage had come with the decision to abandon a role of wearying, demoralizing passivity.

She'd find Joanna Starr herself, and find her first. Wrest from her, ruthlessly if necessary, the key to the whole crazy puzzle. Then he could have her, and she him. Then she herself would be free, free of both of them.

But now in a swift flash she knew there was something wrong somewhere in her careful reasoning. There was no mistaking the stark terror in the eyes of the girl beside her. Once more the burden of protective compassion encompassed her.

"I've got to get out of here." The girl beside her started up from the depths of the chair, but she laid a detaining hand on her arm.

"I know. But you've got to get away without being seen. If Newberger or some of the servants see you trying to slip out they'll detain you 'forcibly' and there'll be a row. That won't do. Be quiet and let me think."

She knew the layout of these brownstone fronts. They were all the same. Basement and first floor doors at the front giving onto the street, an areaway at the rear. But sometimes through the areaway there was an exit.

"Stay here and don't talk," she cautioned, and slid off the arm of the chair. "I'm going to reconnoiter."

The door to the hall had been left open by one of the first applicants to be summoned to an interview with the Newberger lawyer. She slipped through it quietly and paused in the dimly lighted hall. From the drawing room opposite she heard a low murmur of voices, but the door was closed.

She walked cautiously down the hall toward the rear. There was a stairway leading to the basement, and several doors. She opened one of them tentatively. It was a small lavatory with one window looking out onto the rear. But the glass was opaque.

She lifted the window quickly and gazed up and down the rear areaway. There was a door leading from the areaway into the apartment building that backed up against the brownstone front. Made to order.

A few minutes later she slipped back into the room where the others were waiting. There weren't so many now. The lawyer was doing a quick job of weeding them out.

"There's a lavatory and a stairway at the back of the hall," she said in a low voice to the girl in the chair by the window. She told her about the areaway and the door into the building at the rear. "As soon as you can, pretend you're going to the lavatory and slip out and go down the stairs instead. Go out through the areaway and into the apartment at the rear. And from there into the next street."

"Then meet me afterward. A long way from here. The Battery. The first one that gets there will sit on the bench nearest the Aquarium entrance. Only . . ." She hesitated, looked out of the window. He was still there on the other side of the street. Watching. "Only be sure I'm not being followed."

"Are you going to stay and face him down?" There was respect mingled with fear in the question.

"Not if I can help it. But I'll have to leave by the front door with the others."

"Come with me through the rear."

"No, no. Two will attract twice as much attention as one. You'll have a better chance alone. Go on now, quickly." She pushed the girl into action, watched her slip from the room.

And then she waited. It was easy. The others were anxious to take their turns with the lawyer and be done with it. Only she hung back until she was the last to be interviewed.

The lawyer had not, apparently, relished being routed out so early in the morning. He was irritable. And suspicious. He asked her a lot of questions and she invented a lot of answers. Glibly, because she knew she'd be miles away when he got around to checking up on the false address of the false family in Queens which she had given him.

At last he let her go. At the doorway to the Newberger house she paused. Then she opened it cautiously and slipped out onto the stone step. She looked up and down the street and felt a sudden surge of relief. No lounging figure on the opposite curb or anywhere within sight. She walked quickly down the steps and turned to the right toward the downtown subway.

17

The breeze blowing in from the bay was just cool enough to make the sun on the bench nearest the Aquarium feel pleasantly warm. Joanna Starr—the one who had been Helen Varney—sat there and waited.

She looked around to other benches that bordered the path leading to the Aquarium. Idle workers mostly, dropping down for a few minutes' rest before tramping the hard streets in search of nonexistent jobs. A mother or two with children. A few old men.

She glanced at her watch. Eleven-thirty.

She grew restless and got up and strolled to the newsstand on the corner and bought a paper. There was little new in the Steinmark murder case. Little except—

> ... with the revelation that Paul Saniel's real name was originally Paul Starr and that he changed it seven years ago when he went on the stage. Speculation as to whether he is the cousin, brother, uncle or husband of the missing Joanna Starr could not be verified but ...

She put the paper down and let her gaze wander far down the hay speckled with harbor craft.

Presently she glanced at her watch again. Twelve o'clock. There had been plenty of time. She should have been here by now.

She got up and wandered about, always keeping the bench nearest the Aquarium in sight. She scrutinized everyone on the near-by benches again, particularly the older men. Twice she about-faced abruptly and swept the walk behind her with a swift, searching gaze. There was no one.

And yet . . .

Was it her imagination or was it real, that feeling that was growing on her? She quickened her pace. She didn't know why. She couldn't see anyone following.

Still . . .

At one-thirty she knew that it was futile to wait any longer. Either the real Joanna had failed to escape from the Newberger house or, having escaped and come to the Battery, had seen that trailing figure that she herself had been unable to catch in his spying. Had seen him and fled.

Well, no doubt he'd have other clever schemes for "smoking" her out. She'd have to learn to manage her own frustrating role more cleverly after this. Somewhere along the line she'd muffed her end this time. But the next time . . .

A new access of courage filled her, surprised her even. Watching and waiting had begun to destroy her. Now positive action was good. She felt calm and curiously unafraid. Not even of him. It was as if too much terror, too much grinding, eroding dread had finally exhausted all her fear mechanism and it could function no longer.

Only that small, hidden folly of her own emotions still gnawed at the edge of consciousness.

The apartment in the upper Bronx was empty when she got back to it. She had expected that. He couldn't precede her or follow too closely upon her heels. That would be too much of a giveaway.

It was more than an hour before he returned. He was grim and silent as he flung himself into a chair and lit a cigarette with irritated frustration. She smiled to herself, waited for him to start things, to fling accusation in her face. But he was curiously silent and troubled.

All right, if that's the way you want it, that's the way it shall be. Mentally she was repeating his own words. Only, my fine fellow, she added, from now on I'm doing a little watching and trailing of my own.

She lit a cigarette with simulated casualness, took the chair opposite him, opened the paper she had bought at the Battery.

"Were you saying last night something about running away from home and changing your name?" Oh, so casually.

He merely grunted.

"Was your name, before you changed it to Saniel, by any chance—Starr?"

He looked up quickly. Startled. She handed the paper to him and his eyes swiftly took in the story. "All right. So what?"

"Oh, nothing. Rather interesting though. To your friends in Hollywood, I imagine."

He looked puzzled.

"Hollywood—and New York." Her tone was very cool and cutting.

Suddenly his face lighted, then burst into a laugh. A long, hearty one, like that one last night. And all the rancor and frustration cleared from his eyes, replaced by a look of devilment.

"Pinkey, my dear, you're not by any chance thinking of Trudi Hess, are you?"

"Is she the only friend you have in New York?"

He nodded. "That is, of course, besides Jo and you. Or aren't you my friend? You don't act like one a good deal of the time, but maybe that's just because you're trying to suppress that secret passion you have for me."

She got up abruptly and tamped out her cigarette with quick, nervous jerks, and slammed the door behind her as she went into the kitchen. She busied herself at the icebox, getting out butter and cheese and fresh tomatoes, banging utensils with unnecessary loudness.

The table was laid when he came into the kitchen a little while later, and she indicated his place while she stirred a pot on the gas stove.

He reached over and turned off the gas, took the spoon from her hand, laid it aside. An irritated protest rose to her lips, but he held up a restraining hand like a traffic cop.

"I suppose," he said, "I could ask you to tell me all about your little adventure this morning."

He waited, but she made no reply.

"That's what I thought. I don't suppose you'd even tell me whether you saw Jo and whether she was all right." Again that disarming gentleness in his voice.

But still she made no reply.

"Oh, well . . ." He shrugged his shoulders, crossed to the table, sat down in his place and started to munch raw celery while she completed preparations for the meal.

"Glad you mentioned Trudi, though. It gives me an idea."

At the corner of Seventh Avenue and Fifty-ninth Street a girl pulled the late edition of an evening paper out of an ash can and sought a near-by bench across the street in the park. It was getting dark, but there was still enough light for her to read by.

There wasn't anything in the paper about the things that had happened in the Newberger house that morning. The only fresh development in the Steinmark murder case was the removal of Trudi Hess and her retinue from the midtown luxury hotel in which she had been staying to a furnished house. To Number 5 Evergreen Drive, Brooklyn.

But that was just next to Number 3! Next to Hugo Steinmark's!

Trudi Hess had denied a personal interview to the press on the significance of this move; but her father, who had spoken for her to the reporters, reiterated, her statement that she had not seen Paul Saniel since she had come to New York, and her denial that the relationship between them was anything but "pure friendship."

The hands of the girl sitting on the bench reading in the waning light trembled as she pored over the interview.

Later she found another bench, farther into the park, under a tree. She lay down and spread the newspaper over her shoulders and tried to sleep, but it rained.

18

The house at Number 5 Evergreen Drive was bustling with carpenters and painters, and Papa was getting ready to go into town to get another servant from one of the accredited agencies.

And to see the decorators about Trudi's suite. Something in gold and black that would match Trudi's personality. Or at least the personality he was trying so hard to create for Trudi.

Papa sighed. He had so many things on his mind. And he must see the lawyer, too. Now that they were out here where they could keep an eye on the Steinmark house, Papa felt better. It was as if his mere presence next door would keep the house from flying away or getting burned up or being carried off.

The telephone rang, a painter thrust a can of color at him and wanted to know if it was the desired shade, a housemaid reported a shortage of bed linen and Trudi wailed.

"Papa, I'm hungry."

"Trudi, hush."

"But, Papa, I'm not working now. It won't matter if I get just a little fat."

"Trudi, please."

When Papa had gone into town and left her, Trudi roamed moodily about the house and wondered if she'd dare sneak something from the kitchen. She leafed through some of the books she found in the library and wished she had a *True Story* magazine. She tried playing the piano but the painters were at work in the music room.

She wandered into the wide, rear lawn and out to the garage and peered sullenly at the cage where the cheetah was temporarily installed. She wished the cheetah would die or that someone would poison him.

Or was it a her? She didn't know. She didn't care. She just didn't like the cheetah. It was Papa's idea. Something about good publicity. She wished Papa wouldn't get so many ideas about good publicity. Damn Papa

She wished she could have a glass of beer and a piece of apple pie and some roast beef and browned potatoes and ice cream and fruit salad and—

"And might I suggest, madame, some famous Southern fried chicken and corned beef and cabbage and strawberry shortcake with whipped cream?"

She jumped slightly at the voice that had picked up and carried on her thoughts. She turned quickly, startled. They must have come up the driveway, the two people standing there, the middle-aged man with the graying mustache and the tall, dark young girl.

"Madame is dieting, perhaps, and thinks often of food?"

The blue eyes went wide with astonishment at this display of psychic power. "Almost all the time."

"Perhaps madame would like me to bring her some beer and liverwurst?" He was closer now, bowing slightly from the waist in a manner that was at once servile and dignified.

She stared and slow comprehension dawned.

"Paul!"

"Sssh, Trudi! Let's go into the house. I've got to talk to you."

The rooms that were to be Trudi's special suite were located in the south wing and had wide French doors leading directly onto the rear lawn. They stepped through them now, the three of them, and the man closed the doors quietly behind them.

"But—but, *Paul!*"

"Hold it, hold it. And remember the name's Pollock."

"I don't understand."

"Listen, Trudi, you're going to need a lot of new servants in this joint, so I'll be the butler. I have wonderful references. I once played a butler for six months straight in a road company. Salary no object."

"But the lawyer says it's best nobody should know—you know, about it being that you recommended him when Papa was trying to locate August."

He seemed to know what she was getting at despite the disorganized phrasing. He nodded and she went on.

"Papa says so, too. He says it might look bad for you."

He grinned. "Sure. It might look as if I murdered August-Hugo-Steiner-Steinmark so that the last obstacle to our great love would be removed."

"There was a story about that in the paper the other day and Papa was terribly upset."

"Well, Papa should learn that sometimes the best laid plans of mice and press agents turn on 'em and bite 'em."

"What do you mean?"

"Never mind. We're just good friends and all that Hollywood stuff is out. Otherwise if people found out that it was through me that you met Konrad, and that he eventually located Steinmark— Well, it might put a crimp in your plans to collect on the Steinmark estate. Now just do as I say. Hire me as your butler."

She hesitated.

"What would Papa say?"

"Oh, damn Papa!"

"Pau—Pollock!" But even as she protested she found satisfaction in this echo of her own feelings about Papa.

"Hire me as the butler and the girl friend here"—he indicated the tall, dark girl—"as a parlormaid. Her name's Pinkey."

"Well . . ." She temporized. "I'll ask Papa when he gets back. He's in New York for the day."

"Good. It's settled then."

"I didn't say that."

"Yes, but you're weakening. Now listen, Trudi, there's something I want you to do for me. I'll give you the lines and—"

He interrupted himself to toss a dollar bill to the new parlormaid. "Go out to the nearest delicatessen and get a flock of beer and some liverwurst sandwiches."

As she let herself out of the French doors she could hear him rehearsing Trudi.

She was quite a long time finding a delicatessen. There were plenty in the neighborhood; but she passed them preoccupied, feeling her cheeks flushing, angry at herself, glad she was alone.

She was remembering that scene in the apartment the night before. "Interesting to your friends in Hollywood—and New York." And he'd seen right through her and laughed. Because she had fallen for a publicity gag *grande passion* engineered by someone called Papa.

The flush deepened. She turned into a delicatessen and ordered liverwurst sandwiches and beer in a voice which made the bewildered little man behind the counter wonder if he had offended her.

19

There were press cars in the driveway of Number 5 Evergreen Drive and reporters waited on the front lawn.

"What," the *Evening Post* inquired, "is the idea?"

The *World-Telegram* shrugged his shoulders. "I dunno. The city desk got a phone call from some guy here—I think it was the butler—and he said, 'Miss Hess has an important announcement for the press.'" He mimicked the austere voice of a stage butler.

Inside, the house had been cleared of painters and the huge old-fashioned drawing room was softly lighted against the drawn shades. The "butler" looked at his watch. Three o'clock. Too late for the late afternoon editions. But tomorrow morning . . .

He ushered the reporters into the drawing room.

"Miss Hess will be with you in a few moments." He withdrew, closing the doors discreetly behind him. He went to a smaller room about halfway down the hall and pushed open the door.

"O. K., Trudi. They're here. Now remember . . ."

The new parlormaid, the tall, dark girl just hired that morning, left her desultory dusting in the dining room and sidled cautiously out of the door that led onto a long stone terrace that ran the length of the house. There were windows in the drawing room that gave onto this same terrace, and by standing very close against the wall of the house she could hear what was going on. Or at least some of it.

That was Trudi Hess's voice now.

"But of course, gentlemen," she was saying, "of course I know where Paul Saniel is."

There was a stir among the reporters and one of them spoke. "Then why haven't you told the police?"

"Because . . ." There was a brief hesitation. Joanna Starr, pressed close beside the window, tense, listening, could not see, but she imagined accurately the little smile that twisted Trudi Hess's lips. "I haven't told the police, gentlemen, because they haven't asked me."

"But you said—"

"I know, I know. They told me he had disappeared and asked me if I could help them. But they didn't ask me *if I knew where he was*. Careless of them, really." There was a little amused laugh. "Of course at that time I didn't know. But I do now."

"Well, then, where is he?"

Another little laugh. "You'd be surprised."

"Meaning you're holding out on the police."

"Oh, no, not at all. All they have to do is ask me and I'll tell them."

"How about telling us?"

A brief pause. Then, "No, no, gentlemen, I'm afraid not. Not to the newspapers. To the police, yes. The police, and other . . . ah . . . interested parties." There was a peculiar emphasis on this last sentence.

"Did you know his name was Starr and not Saniel?" A reporter shot the question at her.

There was no answer.

"What about these stories from Hollywood about you and Saniel?"

Still no answer, and Joanna Starr guessed correctly that the rehearsal had not included those questions.

Then, "Gentlemen . . . uh . . . Paul Saniel and I are just good friends."

The new parlormaid, pressed close against the side of the house, listening, could almost hear Trudi Hess's hurried exit.

She went back to her dusting. Such a handy occupation, dusting. It could take one almost any place in the house. Any place where one might, perhaps, see or hear—things. She dusted quite a lot that afternoon. She was still at it at five when Otto Hess returned from the city. She was in the hall near Trudi's sitting room. The door to the sitting room was closed, but it wasn't a heavy door.

Not heavy—but very dusty. She bent assiduously to her work and listened to the voices within. There were three of them there. Paul and Trudi and Papa. And there were loud explosive noises, chiefly from Papa.

"I won't have it. I won't. You've got to get out. The police will be here. They'll see you. It'll make trouble. You go, Paul. Immediately. Right away. And, Trudi, what got into you? While I'm gone, you get yourself into such a fix. We must call up the newspapers right away and tell them you don't know anything, you—"

"Too late, Papa, too late." It was Paul Saniel's voice, very cool and calm and in amusing contrast to the irate burbling of Papa.

"You, Paul . . . you . . ." There was another long tirade, and in the tiny intervals while Papa was taking gasping, angry breaths there was the sound of someone chuckling quietly.

". . . and just when Trudi maybe gets all the Steinmark money, you come along and throw monkey wrenches. You're wanted by the police. I could turn you over to them. I could—"

"Listen, Papa." It was Paul Saniel's voice cutting across the tirade. "Tell me something. Tell me, where were you on the night Hugo Steinmark was murdered?"

"Why, I was— What do you mean?"

"Oh, come now, you know what I mean. You were in a few crook melodramas yourself in your day before you stopped being an actor and settled down to being a press agent and wet nurse. Where were you on the fatal night?"

"You mean, Paul—you're saying that maybe I killed—that—" His wrathful sputtering foundered in incoherency.

"Now, now, keep the shirt on. I just asked you. That's all. Maybe you went to the movies."

There was a little pause. Then, "Yes, yes, that's it. I did go to the movies."

"Got any witnesses?"

"No, no. Do you think I advertise it every time I go to the movies? We had just gotten in the day before. I had everything settled. I put Trudi to bed early. I went to the movies. That's the only place where I rest well."

"What picture did you see?"

"Picture? I don't know. I went to sleep. I always sleep best in the movies. You know that, Paul."

Paul Saniel's voice was stern. "Bad," he said, "very bad. You're in a tight spot. I think you'd better consult your lawyer."

You could almost feel the sudden brightening of Papa's tone. "That's a good idea. An excellent idea. I will. Tonight. Before the conference."

"But remember," Paul said, "no word to anyone that I'm here. Not even to your lawyer."

20

A strange conference it was.

A conference tense with hate and distrust and accusation and suspicion. It couldn't be otherwise, including as it did Otto and Trudi Hess; Douane Kingston and his daughter, who claimed to be the wife of the dead Steinmark; and the three lawyers. Jules Konrad representing Trudi Hess; Howland, of the firm of Howland and Storm, acting on behalf of the Steinmark financial interests; and Theron O'Hara, that third legal practitioner who had been introduced into the case by Hugo Steinmark himself.

O'Hara it was who specialized in "pretty confidential personal work," yet who still maintained a puzzling ignorance of the dead Steinmark's intentions. He was there now at the insistence of Konrad. Marc Howland, a hard, shrewd fellow, had protested his presence as unnecessary, but the lawyer for Trudi Hess had been adamant in his demand.

The two of them, Konrad and Howland, did not, it was plain, share in the emotion of the principals. Rather they tried to iron out emotion, to bring the conference down to the dead, practical level of legal compromise and settlement.

Under any circumstances the problem would have been a knotty one. Two women claiming to be the wife of the same man, reaching out for the fortune he had amassed. Two belligerent old men, defending the claims of their young with the fierceness of female tigers.

But the whole thing was made infinitely more complicated by the shadow of murder that lay over them all. Murder and suspicion.

They sat there, the seven of them, their eyes shifting from one to the other, each one wondering, thinking, guessing.

They assembled after dinner about eight o'clock. Konrad came out from town in his own car; O'Hara, by subway and taxi; Douane Kingston and Sylvia Steinmark walked over from the Kingston house. Walked across the lawn of that other house in the middle, where police still stood guard as if to protect it from the two warring camps entrenched on either side of it.

The new butler, strangely enough, did not receive them. He left that to one of the lesser fry on the servants' staff. Queer fellow, he was, all right. Didn't do much work. Not like the new parlormaid at all. She was working all the time, all over the place at once, cleaning, dusting . . . dusting . . .

Still at it, she was, in the lower hall that ran the length of the house, polishing the bric-a-brac of a small table near the entrance to the drawing room, where there was a mumbling of voices. She started slightly when the butler came up quietly behind her.

"Hearing anything interesting, Pinkey darling?" he inquired.

She looked at him but did not answer.

"Who's there?" He nodded in the direction of the drawing room.

"I don't know. I was busy in the kitchen until after they all got here."

While they were talking a bell had rung some place in the house, and now one of the other maids had answered it. She was coming through the dining room bearing a tray with glasses and a siphon and decanter, bound for the drawing room.

"I'll look after this," the butler said, taking the tray from her and giving her a nod of dismissal. He opened the door into the drawing room and went in.

It wasn't more than forty seconds or a minute before a small crash shattered the rumble of talk, and he came hurriedly into the hall with a strange expression on his face. He was breathing quickly. He stared at Joanna Starr.

"What's the matter? What is it?" she demanded.

"I . . . I dropped a glass."

"Yes, I heard."

"Listen," he said, and grabbed her arm. "Don't go in there. Clear out of the front part of the house. Don't let yourself be seen by them." He jerked his head toward the drawing room. "Understand?" And he disappeared in the direction of the kitchen.

For a moment she stared at his receding back. She looked at the door leading into the drawing room like a child guiltily contemplating something forbidden. Then she stuffed her duster into her pocket, looked about to make sure that no one was in the hall who might see her, and slipped out the front door.

Number 5 Evergreen Drive, like the other two houses on the street, was heavily flanked by shrubbery. She bent low in its protecting shadow and rounded a corner of the house. The drawing room, she knew, ran the length of the house and had wide windows giving onto a flagged terrace along the western side. Windows that would be open now in the warm June night.

She made for one of these and crouched down, hiding behind a rattan porch chair. Then, pressing her face against a window casing, she looked into the room, obliquely so that she could see without being seen.

A broken glass on the floor. Seven people sitting there, their faces thrown into planes of light and shadow by the shaded lamps. Her eyes traveled around the circle, halted abruptly. For a moment she stared and felt something teasing the fringes of recollection. Then she remembered. A slow frown creased her brow.

Had Paul Saniel seen the same thing? And was it that which had sent the glass slipping from suddenly nerveless fingers?

She could hear voices.

". . . conference has been suggested as a means of settling things among ourselves, if possible, and avoiding long court litigation."

"But you admit that my client's claims are incontrovertible. We don't really need to deal with you, you know." That must be Konrad, Trudi Hess's lawyer.

"Under the circumstances I think we must all deal with each other." Suave, smooth, with a hint of threat in it. "Mr. Kingston has extensive financial influence in the Steinmark enterprises and could make things very—unpleasant." Kingston's lawyer, probably. The handsome, blond fellow must be O'Hara.

"Perhaps."

"You see, we both have cards in this game."

"Possibly. However, I don't—"

An irascible voice broke in impatiently. "Get down to business. Stop this flilly-flallying. Out with it. Say in plain words what we both want to know."

"And what is that?" Konrad's voice again.

"To put it very bluntly and to stop all this nonsense—how much?"

Both lawyers were shocked at this layman's forthright presentation of the problem.

"Please, Mr. Kingston, let us handle this," Howland protested.

Konrad turned to the large, dark, handsome woman on his left. "Tell me something, Mrs. Stein—" He broke off, hesitating, and then for the first time a new voice entered the mumble of sound. A woman's voice, deep and resonant yet acid.

"Don't be embarrassed, Mr. Konrad. You're not in a court of law now. It won't prejudice your case if you address me as Mrs. Steinmark."

"Yes, I know. Only it is a somewhat—ah—delicate point. But tell me, why did you leave Hugo Steinmark's house three days before he was murdered?"

"I thought we had come here to discuss an out-of-court settlement. Not to play detective."

"Yes, I know. But it might help matters all the way around if you were to explain the reasons for your leaving."

"Very well. First of all, it was to be only temporary."

"The housekeeper said you took all your clothes and personal belongings with you."

"If you prefer the housekeeper's word to mine, why are you questioning me?"

"I'm sorry. Go ahead."

"I left him—just for a little while. Because I was afraid."

"What were you afraid of?"

"I don't know. Him, perhaps. For more than a month he had been nervous and distrait and irritable and sometimes downright savage."

"As if something were on his mind, perhaps?"

"Yes."

"Did he tell you what?"

"No."

"You're sure about that?"

"Do you suppose I would keep anything back? I've nothing to hide."

The lawyer's voice shifted, turned in another direction. "Tell me, O'Hara, did Steinmark before he died reveal to you the nature of any problems that were on his mind?"

"No. I was and still am as completely in the dark as you. I've explained all that to the police."

"Yes, I know. But then, here, now, is, as you might say, off the record. Anything you could tell us might be of inestimable service in reaching an out-of-court settlement. Anything you know . . ."

"But I don't know anything," O'Hara snapped. "If I did I'd say so." He was plainly nettled by the other lawyer's quiet insistence.

"Of course. Sorry." Konrad turned back to the woman. "Tell us a little more, Mrs. Steinmark. Did your husband—"

"He's not her husband. He's mine." It was Trudi Hess, pushing her way into the controversy. Konrad turned to her, placating.

"Yes, yes, that's true. Even Mr. Howland here admits our proofs are incontrovertible." Then to Sylvia Steinmark again, "It's still strange, isn't it? You loved your husband?"

"Of course."

"And yet at a time when he was obviously troubled and distrait, you left him. Very strange. How do you account, Mrs. Steinmark, for the fact that—"

"Stop badgering my daughter," Douane Kingston broke in. "If you want to know it, I was the one responsible for my daughter's leaving Hugo Steinmark's house. I never wanted her to marry him and I'll state frankly that I never wanted her to stay married to him. I moved out here beside them so that I would be at hand always in case of trouble."

"Trouble? What kind of trouble?"

"Why . . . why, just . . . trouble."

"Perhaps, Mr. Kingston, you mean the same kind of trouble that you've always had with your daughter. And with your wife before her."

There were explosive, angry sounds. Kingston started to spring forward. Then Howland cut in, calm but tense.

"Hold on, Mr. Kingston. Wait a minute. That's hitting below the belt, Konrad. It has no relevancy."

"Under the circumstances, Howland, I believe it has."

"I don't see the connection."

"A jury might."

"Now you're being stupid, Konrad. It has nothing to do with—"

"Oh, it *it!*" Sylvia Steinmark's voice, bursting with emotion long restrained, dammed up, poured out in an angry flood. "What do you mean—*it?* Why don't you say what you mean? Both of you. say it for you. My mother committed suicide while temporarily deranged in a private sanitarium.

"I've been in the same sanitarium twice. I'm crazy too—sometimes. Maybe I'm homicidal instead of suicidal. Maybe I killed Hugo Steinmark. Maybe I killed him because I found out he only married me for my father's money so he could get started in business. Maybe I . . . maybe he . . ."

The rising tide of emotion and passion and anguish broke, shattered itself to pieces, sank into the incoherency of mad, hysterical weeping.

There was movement and stir and murmur within the room, everyone talking at once but in low, shocked tones. And a few minutes later the girl crouching behind the rattan chair out on the porch saw two men—one tall and strong and the other white-haired and bent—go out the side door, supporting between them a trembling, babbling creature.

But she didn't see Paul Saniel crouching beside a window, just as she crouched. Only he was on the north side of the house hidden by shrubbery, and she was on the west behind the rattan chair. After the lights in the drawing room had gone out, she slipped into the house through the front door and he through the rear.

Joanna Starr in her small bedroom in the servants' wing lay awake far into the night, her mind still grappling with the strange thing she had seen in the circle of those faces. The house had long since ceased to creak and echo with human sound.

She lit a match and looked at her watch. Two o'clock. She rose and wrapped a dressing gown about her and went to the window.

The servants' quarters were in the rear in a wing that jutted out from the rest of the house, stretching to the west.

There was a faint moon and in its dim light she could see the Steinmark house looming through the trees. She sat there in the darkness staring at certain windows at the rear and knew that it was the library. The library where she and Hugo Steinmark had—

Her thoughts broke off suddenly. She had been staring at the windows of the Steinmark, house, not really seeing them. Now abruptly something brought consciousness to her gaze.

It was a light, very faint, on for a second or two, then off. Like someone with a flashlight, there in the shrubbery by the library. She watched it. Two minutes . . . three . . . She lost track of time. It winked again. Then went off completely.

She felt herself waiting, tense. There was a faint stirring in the bushes that separated the two lawns. A figure darted swiftly, noiselessly, across the brief stretch of treacherous moonlight.

She crept softly to the door of her room, opened it a crack. She heard the stealthy closing of a door somewhere downstairs, the creak of a board, and another and another, getting nearer. Someone was mounting the stairs to the servants' wing. Someone was coming down the hall.

A man, walking softly, softly down the hall to the room at the end to the right. The room which the new butler had taken as his own.

Joanna Starr, standing there in the darkness, waited. Fifteen minutes. Twenty. Then she, too, crept down the hall to that door at the right. It was shut and she put her ear close to the crack. She could hear the deep, regular breathing, the slight snore. Like that other time in the apartment in the upper Bronx.

You were snoring. . . . That's because I have a clear conscience.

Her words and his came back to her now.

But as she crept softly back to her room she was busy with a new train of thought. When the conference had broken up and she had slipped back into the house, she had met him in one of the rear passageways.

His brows had been frowning with thought as he had laid a detaining hand on her arm.

"Tell me something. Just where were you sitting that night in the Steinmark library and where was Steinmark sitting?"

She had been puzzled, but she had told him. Steinmark in the chair behind the desk; she facing him and a little to the right at the side of the desk.

Now in the stillness of the night she remembered this.

She wondered . . .

21

The new butler was nervous.

And a bit snappish. Twice he bawled out one of the maids for answering the telephone. "I'll attend to that," he barked, and his voice was only a little less harsh when he sent the second parlormaid—the ubiquitous duster—to clean up the attic.

He himself stuck close to the main telephone in the butler's pantry and delegated to another the task of serving breakfast to the four in the dining room.

There were Trudi and Papa of course, and the two lawyers, Konrad and O'Hara, who had stayed the night after the abortive conference of the previous evening. There was something queer about the breakfast though. Trudi wasn't eating. She took a sip of orange juice, stirred her coffee fitfully, crumbled toast. And not once did she beg for cream or butter.

Papa seemed a little nervous too, and told the maid quite sharply to leave the morning papers in the drawing room. Only Konrad ate with satisfied unconcern.

But even his poise was ruffled when at last the meal was over and the four of them went into the drawing room. He lit a cigarette, and picked up one of the morning papers and ran his eye over the headlines. Suddenly he sat forward and stiffened.

"What the—"

TRUDI HESS CONCEALS
HIDEOUT OF SANIEL

Papa tried to explain and only made matters worse.

"You mean to say this fellow Saniel is right here in this house, now? I thought I told you—"

"It's all my fault," Papa moaned. "I left Trudi alone. Something always happens when I leave Trudi alone."

Konrad flung down the paper and took a couple of swift strides up and down the room. "Well, the damage is done now. There's no help for it. You know, of course, don't you, that the police will be here any minute now? What are you going to tell 'em?"

"You tell—"

"I've got to be in court at ten, and in the meantime there's the unfinished business of last night with Kingston and Howland."

"Couldn't we put that off?"

"No. They're on their way now. See!"

He jerked his head in the direction of the window that gave onto the side lawn. Howland and Kingston were approaching, crossing the Steinmark yard and slipping through the little gate in the shrubbery that separated the two places.

Kingston looked worn and haggard and his footsteps were dragging. He gave a brief nod that included Otto Hess and the others, and dropped into a chair. Howland closed the door into the hall and the conference of the night before was resumed.

But there were absences. There was no dark, anguished woman giving way to the babblings of hysteria. There were no hidden listeners crouching beneath the windows. And Trudi of the wide, innocent blue eyes wandered restlessly about the house.

In the butler's pantry Paul Saniel sat beside the telephone. Waiting. Tense.

In the attic Joanna Starr waited, too. Thinking of that dark figure that had prowled about the Steinmark house in the early hours of the morning.

Thinking of that, and of the thing she had seen in the circle of faces in the drawing room. Again she wondered if Paul Saniel had seen the same thing, and had dropped a glass with the sudden impact of recognition.

A vague outline was beginning to form.

Her mind wandered back to another morning and the tragic figure of Charles W. Newberger standing in the doorway to a little anteroom filled with girls. *There has been some mistake . . . something queer.*

A door was jerked open and she started violently. It was Paul Saniel. He grabbed her arm, pulled her roughly after him.

"Get going!" He was running down the stairs from the attic, drawing her with him into the lower hall.

"What—" she began.

"Quiet! Here, this way!"

"Where are we going?"

"Shut up and save your breath. Follow me."

She followed him down the back stairs into the basement, then up a small flight of steps to the drying yard of the laundry, separated by tall bushes from the rest of the lawn. As they emerged into the open air, her ears caught a new sound. Faint and far away but unmistakable. Sirens. Police sirens, wailing, shrill, getting nearer.

He paused suddenly, looked back. She followed his gaze and a swift picture printed itself on her mind.

Kingston and Howland crossing the Steinmark lawn to the Kingston house. The lawyer, Konrad, getting into his car parked in the driveway. The other lawyer, O'Hara, nowhere to be seen. And at an upstairs window she thought she caught a glimpse of Trudi Hess peering out.

"Duck down." He pushed her roughly through a hole in the hedge at the rear. There were empty lots and heavy trees behind the three houses. On one side lay Shore Road and the bay. On the other, the maze of South Brooklyn apartment houses. Somewhere in that maze there was a subway station.

As they emerged from the trees he slowed down their pace. Both of them were panting.

"Walk quickly but don't run," he snapped. "Don't attract attention."

They could hear the sirens behind them, screeching, mingling their wails with the heavy exhaust of a police motorcycle escort. But soon their quick steps left the sound behind. It was lost entirely as they ran down the subway stairs.

They just missed a train and he swore softly.

"Maybe a taxi . . ."

"Subway's quicker. Taxi in traffic—get held up—we'd never get there."

"Where's there? Where are we going?"

He looked about quickly. There was no one else on the platform. He pulled her down to a seat, spoke in low, quick words.

"She telephoned, just now, just a few minutes ago."

"Who?"

"Joanna."

"Oh."

"She saw Trudi's statement in the paper—about knowing where I was."

"And grabbed at the bait?"

"Yes. But cagey. She's scared. She recognized my voice, but she's scared of some kind of a trap. I gave her exact directions. She's to come in at the eastern Forty-second Street entrance to Grand Central and walk down the ramp to the information desk. That's where we meet."

A train roared into the station and they boarded it and found seats. She glanced out of the side of her eyes at the man beside her. His fingers beat a nervous tattoo on one knee. His face was tense. But there was a light in his eyes, an eagerness. He was going to meet that other Joanna at last! *His* Joanna!

She felt a fierce jolt as if her heart were turning over.

At Grand Central they struggled out of the train, lost themselves in the heavy stream of human traffic, followed the green lights to the upper level. At the information desk she looked at the clock. Five minutes to eleven.

"I said eleven-fifteen on the phone," he explained. "I knew it would take a little while for us to get here."

She leaned against an empty window of the information desk. He paced back and forth restlessly. The hands of the clock above them moved slowly. Eleven-five . . . ten . . .

Now, in just five minutes she told herself, she would come, that other Joanna. No, no, *the* Joanna, the "darling" Joanna. In just five minutes more she would be Helen Varney again, and the puzzle would be resolved by that other Joanna who held the key. And *he* . . .

Around them people rushed for trains, and redcaps hustled luggage, and mobs at the information desk demanded the track for the eleven-seventeen to Larchmont and the next train for Stamford, and excited vacation-bound children laughed shrilly. And street traffic rumbled, and all the sights and sounds were mingled and lost themselves, merging with the great din of the city, humming, rattling, roaring in one mighty stream of sound.

In just five minutes now . . . no, no, less than five minutes. In just . . .

The steady stream of sound was broken. Suddenly. A swift rat-tat explosion and then another and another.

An automobile backfiring perhaps.

But at the entrance at the top of the ramp that led from Forty-second Street there was a new, agitated swirling of the traffic. There were shouts and the long shrill blast of a whistle; someone screamed. The entrance was clogged now with people, some struggling and fighting to get away, others pushing forward in sudden excitement.

Paul Saniel stopped his nervous pacing. He was standing beside her now, watching the commotion at the door. He was breathing quickly, his eyes questioning the commotion.

Then suddenly he sprang forward.

"*Oh, good God!*"

She felt herself pulled along with him, dodging their way up the ramp, making for that milling mass at the entrance.

"Not this way! Everybody stand back!" It was a policeman's voice above the hubbub.

"I said stand back." There was a rough hand on Paul Saniel's shoulder.

"But, officer—"

"If you've got to get out in such a hurry use another exit. Everybody away from this door."

He was reinforced now by a whole squad of police, pushing back the struggling mass, pushing it down the ramp into the rotunda of the station, roping off the exit."

"But, *officer—*"

"*Stand back!*"

They couldn't buck the mass retreating under the pressure of the line of blue uniforms. She felt his hand on her arm again, pulling her with him, disentangling them from the mob. They made for the exit through the main waiting room weaving through the traffic like football players dodging interference.

But at Forty-second Street there was another mob and more police and ropes and shouting. There was the wail of a siren. Not the shrill screech of a police car, but the softer, ominous siren of an ambulance.

And there was an excited boy—twelve perhaps—the center of an avid group. They could hear jerking, half-finished sentences.

"I was right there in a doorway and this dame was coming along Forty-second from Lexington, and then the shooting started—from a car close to the sidewalk. There was two men in it—and she drops and—"

"What did she look like?"

The boy blinked at the sudden interruption, at the fierce clutch of the man's hand on his shoulder, at the eyes blazing behind the question.

"Why . . . uh . . . just a dame."

"Young or old?"

"Young—and good looking."

"Light or dark?"

"Oh . . . I . . . sorta like *her.*" He pointed to the girl beside the man. "Sorta tall and dark."

The clutching hand slipped from the boy's shoulder. And the soft wail of the ambulance grew fainter as it made its way toward Bellevue on the East River.

22

They had gone immediately to Bellevue, of course.

The great, rambling pile of the city's hospital had towered above them like a mountain to be scaled, a mountain whose approaches were guarded by the huge boulders of hospital rule and routine.

And police. For the bullet-riddled body of the girl that had been lifted from the Grand Central pavement had soon been identified as that of the missing Joanna Starr.

The early afternoon papers had blazoned it across the front pages, where it fought for space with the story of the butler missing from the household of Trudi Hess. The butler who called himself Pollock but who was Paul Saniel whose real name was Starr, too.

Otto Hess had made the best of a bad bargain, and a very good best it was at that. Trudi had been the innocent victim of treachery, the tool of terror. The perfidious Paul had come to her house at a time when he knew that she did not have the protecting presence of Papa. He had threatened her, terrified her, until in panic she had done what he had demanded.

They read the story together, the two of them, sitting on a bench along the East River water front that flanked the hospital.

"Tell me," he demanded when they had finished, and his voice was hoarse and strained, "tell me again just where all those extensions were."

And so she went over for the second time a list of the telephone extensions in the Hess house, a list she had unconsciously compiled in her dusting peregrinations. One in the drawing room,

147

another in the front hall, a third in the library in the rear, one up-stairs in one of the bedrooms.

"Practically lousy with 'em," he said. "Now tell me again what you saw that last time you looked back."

And she described that brief picture that had printed itself upon her mind as they had fled that morning across the drying yard and through the back hedge.

Trudi Hess at an upstairs window. Kingston and Howland going across the Steinmark lawn to the Kingston house. Konrad getting into his car.

"How about O'Hara?"

"I didn't see him any place. Nor Papa."

"But all of 'em were in the house when that call came through. And an extension around every corner. I should have thought of that." He was bitter in self-accusation.

"Funny," she said after a moment. "Not quite all of them."

"What do you mean?

"Sylvia Steinmark."

"Yeah."

"And Newberger."

He nodded, then reached for the newspaper again. "And ac-cording to this at eleven-fifteen this morning Konrad was pleading a case in the Court of General Sessions, Section 2; Theron O'Hara was at his office on East Twenty-fourth Street; Papa was miles away in Brooklyn telling tall stories to the newspapers; Howland was still at the Kingston house with Douane Kingston."

Over his shoulder she reread part of the newspaper story.

> No trace of the killer's car has been found yet. The
> getaway was made, it is believed, via the ramp lead-
> ing to the Park Avenue overpass that flanks Grand
> Central. In the confusion and near riot which fol-
> lowed the shots, no one . . .

They sat in heavy silence for a little while, their eyes gazing unseeing at the slow-moving river. A boy came along with the day's final edition. Paul Saniel tossed him a coin and snatched a paper nervously. He took one glance at the small boxed bulletin on the front page, and the hand holding the paper shook.

> An official bulletin from Bellevue at two-thirty this afternoon described the condition of Joanna Starr as "very grave," and little hope was held for recovery.

His head dropped into his hands and a soft, tragic sound escaped his lips.

She picked up the paper and took in the boxed bulletin with one swift glance. She laid a gentle hand on his arm. His other hand crept up to meet hers, clasped it hard and trembling. Then abruptly he rose from the bench.

"Where are you going?"

"There. I've got to see her. I've got to get in."

"Don't be a fool. The police are there. They'll nab you right away."

"Yes, I know." He was walking rapidly now toward the emergency ward entrance halfway down the block. Her hand was still on his arm, attempting to hold him back. He tried to shake it off.

"I'm going with you," she said.

"No, no."

"I'm going." There was steel and granite in her voice. He protested again, but his protests shattered themselves futilely against her resolve.

"The police haven't got me spotted as they have you. They don't know me or what I look like."

"*They* don't, but—" He jerked up short, grabbed both her hands. She met his gaze with level eyes.

"I know. I mean I think I know. It—"

She broke off. A woman was passing, eying them in questioning surprise—these two standing there on the edge of the sidewalk, caught up in some strange intensity of emotion.

"Not here," he said under his breath.

They resumed their quick steps toward the emergency ward entrance. But before they reached it she jerked him to a stop again.

"The money—the Newberger ransom money! Have you got it on you?"

"Yes."

"Give it to me, quickly. If you're arrested they'll find it on you."

"Yes, I know."

"Then give—"

"And then maybe they'd find it on you. No." And his resolve was as hard and granitelike as hers.

They went in the emergency ward entrance and found themselves in a long hall. At the other end of it they could see a room with a desk and a nurse in charge.

"Listen," he said softly, "we go in separately as if we didn't belong together. If they ask who you are, say you're a reporter. You know, one of the sob sisters, trying to crash through to Joanna Starr. The most they'll do is throw you out. Understand?"

She nodded.

They went down the long corridor. He was slightly in the lead. A feeble electric light in the ceiling did little to dispel the gloom of the waiting room. At the right of the nurse's desk there was another corridor with evenly spaced doors opening onto it. And in front of several of the doors there were uniformed patrolmen. At one of the doors there were two, sitting in silent, ominous guard.

At the left there were some benches and chairs. A few people. Waiting. A woman, worn and work-weary, shabbily dressed. Probably some wounded gangster's mother. Three nondescript men. Two of them sitting close together, talking in low tones. Gangster pals, maybe. The third one, sitting apart, leafing a tattered movie magazine nervously, looked as if he'd give his soul for a smoke.

Paul Saniel walked up to the desk. The nurse eyed him hostilely.

"I want to see Joanna Starr." His voice was firm and clear and there was a certain challenging defiance in it. The other people in the waiting room looked up, startled.

The nurse's hard eyes didn't falter, but her hand pressed a signal button on the edge of the desk. One of the patrolmen in the corridor at the right rose from his chair and approached the nurse's desk.

"Someone to see Joanna Starr," she said quietly.

The patrolman looked at Paul Saniel.

The people in the waiting room were suddenly motionless.

The girl standing just inside the door waited.

"What do you—" The patrolman started to speak, then halted abruptly as he caught the full light on Paul Sallies face. He stared. But not with the casual carelessness of the layman. He scrutinized the face before him with eyes trained by experience to see past subterfuges and artful trickery.

"What's your name?"

"Paul Saniel."

"Yeah. I thought so. Come with me."

The eyes of the girl beside the door never left the figure that the patrolman shepherded before him. The two men almost brushed her clothes as they passed her. But Paul Saniel stared woodenly ahead of him. She watched them disappear and her breath seemed to stop in her throat.

"Were you here to see someone?"

The voice of the nurse at the desk broke through. She started, remembering suddenly. She got a grip on herself. She advanced to the desk, trying to simulate hard-boiled, newspaper confidence.

"I'm from the *World-Telegram*. I'm here to get a story about Joanna Starr. Can you tell—"

"I'm not supposed to discuss matters with the newspapers." The nurse spoke crisply. "And anyway," she added slyly, "you're a little late. Another woman reporter from the *Telegram* was just here a few minutes ago."

"Oh." She tried to cover confusion and did it badly.

"Show 'em your press card, sister." It was a man's voice from the other side of the room, a voice whose sympathies were obviously with her confusion.

"I . . . uh . . . I'm sorry, but it's . . . I lost it."

She turned and walked slowly from the room, down the long corridor to the exit, conscious of having muffed it badly.

23

She was alone.

There were seven million people in the city around her, eating, talking, riding in subways, sitting in parks, dodging traffic. They brushed against her and bumped into her, and the roar and the din of their living filled her ears, and she was buffeted and pushed along in the swift stream of their motion.

Still she was alone. More alone than she had ever been before in her life.

The hot summer night settled upon the city like a stifling blanket, and sent its millions into the streets in search of surcease from the heavy, humid air. Like that other night in the two mean bedrooms under the baking roof of a brownstone rooming house. That night it had all started.

She tried to think back, to reckon how long ago that was. Nine days in time. But life was measured not by time alone but by the fullness of it.

She walked. But without conscious objective. The brain that furnishes direction was sorting out crazy pieces made up of chance words, a look here, an intonation there, forming a pattern that was slowly emerging from the tumult of those nine days.

She was alone. But she had things to do.

She looked at her watch. Ten o'clock. More than six hours since she had walked out of Bellevue and left behind, involved in the octopus tentacles of the law, the man whose presence had been so fraught with some unknown, creeping menace. At first anyway.

Until he had found out that the real Joanna was still real and still living. And then menace had given way to the unnerving giddiness of relief. He had been gay almost. And protecting, too. Protecting her. She knew it now.

Slowly the crazy pieces fell into place and the vague outlines of the pattern became clearer.

She looked about her and for the first time was conscious of the pushing, sweating city that surrounded her. Conscious of the fact that she was tired, so tired, with hours of directionless walking. And hungry.

She stopped at a tiny diner and got a sandwich and an iced drink. She counted the money in her purse. Four dollars and some change. She hoped it would be enough. She sought a place to sleep in a cheap hotel on a dimly lit street off Broadway.

The great Steinmark murder case was practically solved. Just a few minor details to clear up.

Joanna Starr who had once been Helen Varney read the denouement as she ate breakfast in another cheap diner with the morning *Gazette* propped up in front of her.

The *Gazette* was original. It wasn't satisfied with routine police handouts. It had ideas of its own. And now one of them sprawled across the front page in screaming type.

Lance Sheriton, ace detective story writer, known to millions for his astute tales of crime, had been hired to write an exclusive "reconstruction" of the case.

He began by pointing out that Paul Saniel, since his arrest the previous day in the waiting room of Bellevue Hospital, had refused to talk. Only once had he broken his silence, when he demanded that he be allowed to consult a lawyer, and had in turn selected Jules Konrad, Theron O'Hara and Marc Howland.

> All three are already involved in the case through their representation of the Steinmark and Hess interests. All three when contacted refused the case. Konrad with bewilderment, O'Hara with indignation, and Howland with curt hauteur.

But Paul Saniel's silence had not cut off speculation, particularly after the receipt by New York police of a wire from the Los Angeles and Hollywood authorities confirming the fact that Saniel had been absent from his Hollywood apartment for three weeks during the previous September.

On September 6 Paul Saniel left his apartment. Six days later, on September 12, Ronald Newberger was kidnaped from the Newberger estate at Central Islip. On September 13 Charles W. Newberger received a demand for $50,000 ransom money together with detailed instructions for the delivery of the money to the kidnapers. *Do not get in touch with the police or else* . . . This was the command attached to the kidnap note.

It will be remembered that he was instructed to place the money in a suitcase and leave it at the Grand Central station checkstand nearest the Forty-second and Vanderbilt Avenue exit. He was then to walk away, down Forty-second Street to Broadway. On the northeast corner of Broadway and Forty-second Street he was to pull his handkerchief from his pocket and "accidentally" let fall to the pavement the check for the suitcase. And then to walk on—*without looking back.*

Charles W. Newberger followed these directions to the letter. Only one thing he did in defiance of instructions. He made a memorandum of the serial numbers of the one hundred $500 bills. Made it secretly, confided in no one, not even in his most trusted advisers.

On September 20 the dead body of Ronald Newberger was found in the Long Island swamps. The suitcase had long since been taken from the Grand Central checkstand. And on September 26 Paul Saniel returned to his Hollywood apartment.

The subsequent "reconstruction" of the case required all the devious skill of the famous Lance Sheriton. Like most *Gazette* writers, he made use of sly innuendo, clever juxtaposition of fact, cunning insinuation, but always stopped short just this side of the law of libel. But the inference was there.

Joanna Starr—the real one—and Paul Saniel had been accomplices. With her help the Newberger child had been enticed away from a careless nursemaid and murdered. The ransom demand had been made on Charles W. Newberger and the money collected.

But when the dead body of the child had been discovered in the Long Island swamp, Charles W. Newberger had gone to the police with the serial numbers of the ransom money. These had been immediately broadcast, and the kidnapers knew that in one respect at least they had been double-crossed.

Their fifty thousand dollars was "hot money." They dared not spend it until some distant future when the trail had grown cold and the memory of man had forgotten. And so they lay low, Paul Saniel to return to Hollywood, Joanna Starr to remain in New York guarding the "hot money."

But kidnaping was not the only string which Saniel had to his criminal bow. Blackmail could be profitable too, if the opportunity offered. And Trudi Hess, international film star, with the secret of her marriage, offered just that opportunity.

As her director Saniel was, of course, in a position to know much of that secret, so that, even while Trudi Hess through her New York attorney was searching for her husband, Saniel and his accomplice, Joanna Starr, had conducted an independent investigation which had led them, more than a month ago, to Hugo Steinmark.

But Steinmark, the story pointed out, was not the easy mark the blackmailers had anticipated. He had resolved to fight fire with fire, and to that end did some detective work of his own. Just how he discovered that his two blackmailers were the kidnapers and murderers of Ronald Newberger was not known. But it was obvious that he possessed this knowledge and was prepared to use it to the fullest extent.

He made an appointment with Joanna Starr for the evening of Thursday, June 4. The police had the note in his own handwriting confirming the date. And he had an appointment with Charles W. Newberger on the morning of Friday, June 5. But on the evening of Thursday, June 4, he was murdered.

And right here Lance Sheriton came up against a tough nut that not even the mighty brain that had launched a dozen best sellers could crack. But he was not without theories.

The "lady in lilac"! She had appeared at the house of Hugo Steinmark on the night of June 4, had shot him while Paul Saniel had crouched by the French doors at the west end of the library. And then she had disappeared.

The Sheriton assumption was that the real Joanna Starr had finally come to the point where she was fed up with the whole dark, devious business of kidnaping, murder and blackmail, tired of being the unwilling tool of Saniel.

And she had felt herself betrayed by Saniel's rumored attentions to the glamorous Trudi Hess. She had revolted and sold out the man who had been her partner in crime.

But at the last moment she hadn't been able to summon the courage to go through with it. The "lady in lilac" had taken over at this point, and taken the Newberger ransom money with her. Had assumed the name of Joanna Starr, lived at Joanna Starr's room at the Waldorf-Astoria, received her mail, answered her telephone calls, and kept her appointment with Hugo Steinmark.

When Paul Saniel realized that he had been betrayed he knew that there could be no peace or safety for him until Joanna Starr was put out of the way, and so one last bloody chapter had been written the previous morning at eleven-fifteen at the Grand Central station.

This attempted murder demonstrated, according to Lance Sheriton, the possibility of a gangster tie-up, for witnesses had testified that the shots had come from a sedan carrying two men. But the job had been muffed. Joanna Starr might live, although the issue was still in grave doubt according to Bellevue physicians. Yet even that slim possibility of life was an ever threatening menace to Paul Saniel, so with unprecedented boldness he had walked into Bellevue Hospital the previous afternoon to finish up the job. Probably with only his bare hands, for a police search revealed no weapons.

Only forty-nine thousand five hundred dollars in Newberger ransom money.

But there were two final pertinent questions which Lance Sheriton posed to his readers and left unanswered.

> Did he get it from the "lady in lilac"? And, if so, what is the relationship of these two to each other and to the woman who lies dying, perhaps, in Bellevue Hospital?

The girl eating breakfast on the high stool in the dingy diner laid down the paper and stirred her coffee meditatively. It was all there. A few of the details missing perhaps, a few with slight inaccuracies. But the broad general outline matched the pattern that had slowly taken shape in her own mind.

But with two exceptions.

She drank the last of her coffee, paid her ten cent check, went out into the early morning sunshine, and started walking. At the Pennsylvania station information booth she asked for the next train to a small, remote New Jersey station.

"There's only one out train a day that stops there. Leaves here at three-forty-seven this afternoon."

She turned away with a sense of frustration. Three-forty-seven. That was hours away. Then she brightened. That would give her time to go over to the Public Library. She emerged into the roaring traffic of Seventh Avenue and started walking east.

The newspaper room of the library was almost deserted so early in the morning, and she got the back number she asked for with no delay. She took it to a far corner of the room near the window and spread it out where the daylight would fall on it. Spread out that page she had first read in the dim kerosene light of a dark little cabin in the Jersey hills.

Paul Saniel and Joanna Starr staring up at her from the photographs on the front page. ". . . identified as Joanna Starr of the Eighty-seventh Street address, but not the Joanna Starr who was at the Steinmark house . . ."

When she returned the paper to the desk she asked for back numbers for the period of September 12 to 20 of the previous year.

The Newberger kidnaping was the big story for that period. Column upon columns of it. But the girl wading through the press barrage seemed intent on one angle only of the case.

> . . . as the instructions to Newberger read. He was to come into New York from his estate at Central Islip and place the one hundred $500 bills in a suitcase, under the lining of the bottom. The lining was then to be smoothed back into place so that the bills would not be visible. He was then to fill the suitcase with ordinary articles of masculine apparel—shirts, underclothing, shaving accessories, handkerchiefs. This he did and when . . .

The late afternoon sun slanted against the western wall of the little wooden station as the local puffed to a grinding stop and discharged a passenger. It was past six o'clock and she had had nothing to eat, but the wide place in the road boasted not even a diner.

The local grocery store was still open though, and there were crackers and cheese and fruit. She tucked the paper sack under her arm and started down the tiny street that tapered off into a deep rutted road winding through the woods up into the hills.

There was a lightness, a *lift*, to her steps even as she climbed the difficult road; and the stone that had been her heart had dissolved, leaving an excited buoyancy in its place. She did not hurry. There was no need. There was time, plenty of it, and there was a sureness now, a confidence in what she was doing that made the groping fears and alarms of the last nine days seem foolish.

It was dusk when she reached the cabin. It stood squat and silent and alone; and she sank down on its stone stoop with a thankful sigh, puffing slightly from the long climb. She ate her crackers and cheese and fruit and watched darkness slowly settle upon the woods, and listened to the crickets and owls and tree toads wakening to the night.

At last she rose, tried the door. It pushed inward easily, for Paul Saniel had broken the lock that night when they had first come there. Groping her way through the thicker darkness of the cabin, she found the coal oil lamp and matches on the kitchen table. A circle of feeble light pierced the blackness. She carried the light into the bedroom and set in on the dresser and threw back the chintz curtains that formed a makeshift closet.

And there it was.

The thing she had come all the way from New York to retrieve. The heavy brown leather suitcase which she had packed before that swift flight from the Waldorf. The suitcase which that other Joanna had seemed to think important.

Take care of it—I mean the heavy brown one. You may need it someday. Need it badly. The words of the other girl came back to her now.

She turned the case on end and looked at the initials stamped on the leather and nodded to herself in some secret confirmation. Then she lifted the case onto the bed and emptied it of the few bits of clothes and toilet articles it still contained. With flattened hands and alert, sensitive fingers she felt the lining. And again there was that nod of secret confirmation.

The lining was loose. She inserted a fingernail under one corner and pealed it back. Bringing the lamp closer, she slowly examined each inch of the space laid bare. In one corner there was a tiny triangular piece of paper torn along its base, still adhering to the glue of the bottom. A piece that was neither of the lining nor of the canvas beneath it. On it were fragments of green, engraved scrollwork and half of what seemed to have been a figure. The figure O. It was a corner torn from a bill.

A five hundred dollar bill! This was the suitcase in which Charles W. Newberger had placed the fifty thousand dollars kidnap ransom money. She had known it would be. Now it was here, beneath her hands, confirmation of the pattern, a weapon of defense and exposure, the key to all the dark business of these last incredible days.

She heaved a great sigh, like one who has at last achieved a high eminence from which the land below lies plain to the eye.

She reached for her handbag and took out a pack of cigarettes and struck a match.

But she didn't light the cigarette, The hand holding the match halted abruptly in mid-air.

There had been a sound. Not a tree toad or a cricket or branches swaying in the soft wind. But another sound, one not of the night and the woods. The match burned out and the cigarette fell from her hand.

It was behind her. Over by the window. Suddenly she stiffened. She didn't breathe. She just stood there, nerving herself to turn around. She put out a hand and clutched the bedpost for support.

Then slowly she turned.

There, framed in the small square of the window, was a face—a man's face, and the look on it was black and evil.

24

The man swung a leg over the sill and thudded softly into the room. Unhurried, leisurely. He even smiled a little. A crooked smile.

She had known fear before. In some dim past she had trembled, grown cold. But all that was pale and shadowy beside the emotion that gripped her now. Emotion compounded of all the panic and terror of a lifetime, distilled into an essence of pure horror, surging through her veins, paralyzing every fiber and cell.

She couldn't move. She couldn't cry out or scream. She could only stand there clutching the bedpost, her eyes staring . . . wide . . .

"Sleepwalking?" His voice snapped the taut string that held her upright. Her knees went suddenly weak and she slid down onto the bed.

"If you don't mind," he said, and there was exaggerated, mocking politeness in his tone, "I'll take charge of this."

He lifted the suitcase beside her from the bed, snapped it shut, set it under the window from which he had just come.

"You were about to light a cigarette? Allow me."

He produced his own case, held it out to her. It was then for the first time she saw that he was wearing gloves. In the warm June night while tiny beads of perspiration gleamed on his forehead.

Wearing gloves!

As the full implication of it struck her, the terror that was in her veins congealed. Wearing gloves that subsequently there might be no telltale fingerprints. And offering her a cigarette with formal courtesy.

Suddenly she wanted to laugh crazily, shrilly. It was like a play she'd seen once with a general of British redcoats chatting amicably with a Continental he was about to have hanged.

"Won't you . . ." she began, and the crazy laughter played around the edges of her voice. "Won't you . . . sit down?" In the old English-drawing-room-comedy drama manner.

He moved a chair from the side wall and placed it directly in front of her; straddled it, leaning his arms against the back so that his eyes were on a level with hers.

"Do you mind telling me," he said, "how you happened to be in Jo's room in the Waldorf when I called?"

She remembered now. That first morning at the Waldorf. On the telephone. *You weren't trying to run away from me, were you?* Her numbed brain responded to a quick flash. Later, that afternoon when she had returned from shopping. *A gentleman to see you, Miss Starr. A Mr. Hutton.*

He'd been there then. Giving a false name, waiting until he was paged but not answering to the paging. Just sitting there some-where, waiting, watching, to confirm the suspicions of the morn-ing. *Is this you, Joanna?*

"You haven't answered my question," he reminded. "How did you happen to meet up with Jo?"

"I . . . she . . ." No use talking now. No use anything now. No use even to stall for time. The cabin was beyond sight or sound of human help. She could scream her throat out. And the dark woods would not give off even the comfort of an echo.

She had complained that life was dull and ordinary. She had wanted to live excitingly, thrillingly! Now she was going to die. To die with his gloved hands at her throat—or a knife—or a gun. No, not a gun. Not like that other time.

"It was you—wasn't it—that night at the Steinmark house out-side the window? And you tossed the gun?"

His lips twisted into a hard smile. "Just a gag, sister. Just a gag. And how you fell for it! Women are dumb. You can always figure out their reactions ahead of time. Maybe that'll be a lesson to you. Next time you—"

"Next time?"

"Sorry, my mistake. There won't be any next time."

He moved toward her. His face was clouded now, and the cool, confident smile left it. He had risen from the chair and pushed it roughly aside. There was hunted fear in his eyes.

Hugo Steinmark had found him out, and Steinmark had died. Joanna Starr had found him out, and been riddled with bullets. And now . . . There was one other person who had found him out. He stood over her, gazing at her darkly, breathing heavily.

She shrank back against the bed. She felt his hands on her shoulders, creeping up to her throat. She felt his eyes coming close, closer . . . hands tight . . .

She struggled, writhed, kicked, clawed, like an animal trapped and doomed who yet fights on through primal instinct alone. She tried to scream and the cry was throttled in her throat . . . choking . . . pounding in her ears, pounding . . . pounding . . . with crazy zig-zagging prisms of light . . . blinding with brightness and blackness . . . choking . . . gasping . . . And a fearful crashing and thunder and shouting . . . and voices . . .

Human voices . . . somewhere . . . some . . . And air pouring into her throat . . . strong arms about her . . . voices . . .

"Pinkey!"

And then one last quick flash—Jules Konrad struggling impotently in the grip of two men, his gloved hands lashed together with the steel of handcuffs.

"Pinkey darling!"

The words, and the voices, and the strong arms that enveloped her eased her softly into the blessed relief of unconsciousness.

.

25

"But, Papa, I don't understand."

"Look, Trudi, it's all here in the papers. Can't you read?" Papa was upset, terribly upset, and in his agitated pacing he trampled on the newspapers that were scattered all about.

"But he was such a nice man. Paul recommended him."

"Yes, yes, but Paul had never seen him. He didn't know he was such a scamp."

"Why did he keep saying we mustn't say anything about Paul recommending him?"

"Because then people would want to know how Paul knew about him. And then it would come out that Paul was Joanna Starr's brother, and Konrad was afraid that that would hitch him up with the Steinmark murder."

"But he did find August, Papa, and now we'll get all that money."

"Yes, yes, I know. But we wouldn't have seen any of the money if other things hadn't happened. He was going to blackmail August himself. He never even told us he'd found August until after he'd murdered him."

"If what other things hadn't happened?"

"August found this Joanna and forced it out of her about the Newberger business. This Joanna—"

"You mean the one that was the maid here?"

"No, no. The one that got shot."

"Did Konrad shoot her?"

"One of his gang did. He was the front of a notorious gang, the one that kidnaped the little Newberger boy."

"But he was Mr. Newberger's lawyer."

"Yes, yes. That's why he was in a strategic position. He was a very wicked man, Trudi, but a very smart one."

"Smarter than you, Papa?"

Papa was too agitated to feel the barb in the simple question, but the complacency with which it was uttered added irritation to his general upset. "But, Trudi," he burst out, "can't you understand? Don't you realize that he might have murdered *us?*"

Trudi was singularly unmoved, even a bit smug. "But, Papa, it was your idea, finding August. I never cared whether I ever saw him again or not."

"I know, I know. But I thought maybe he'd . . . perhaps . . . Oh, anyway, there would be some publicity in it."

"Well," said Trudi as she surveyed the scattered papers, "there was."

"I know, I know, but I don't know whether it's the right kind." Papa was almost weeping. "It's bad getting mixed up in a murder case even if you're innocent. Bad for an actress. Oh, my poor Trudi, maybe I shouldn't . . . maybe I've . . ."

"Look, Papa, don't you think you'd feel better if we were to have some beer and liverwurst?"

"Trudi, *liebchen!*"

Joanna Starr—the one who had been Helen Varney—sat at a desk at headquarters between Inspector Frye and Detective Homer, and opposite her there was a third man with pencil and shorthand notebook.

"And how did Steinmark act when you arrived there Thursday night?"

"He was puzzled of course. A strange woman using a name that he knew belonged to someone else."

"But what did he say? How did he treat you?"

"Very courteously—and cautiously. But I could see he was leading me on to do most of the talking. He was trying to find out what it was all about without committing himself."

"And what did you say to him?"

"I'd planned an act beforehand. And rehearsed my lines. After all, I had to give him a demonstration of what I could do if he'd give me a job. I had made a pretty good scene out of it. First, rather cool and superior and bold. Showing off what I could do with arrogance and restraint. 'You're rather puzzled, I imagine, aren't you?' You know, that sort of line.

"Then I planned to abandon coolness and arrogance and work into a really good emotional scene, telling just what I thought of managers and the damnable way they slam the door in the face of new talent. After that I was going to— But then, of course, I never got that far."

"You mean you were interrupted?"

"Interrupted?" She laughed. "That's rather an understatement. And anyway it was Steinmark who was interrupted. From there on it isn't awfully clear in my mind."

"That's understandable, but recall as best you can."

"There was a shot. And Steinmark's face twisted in a horrible grimace. He pulled himself up from the chair and just stood there for a moment, swaying and groping with one hand.

"I felt something hit my lap. I grabbed hold of it without really realizing what it was. I must have risen from the chair then and advanced a few steps toward him, because when he finally fell forward the hand that had been pawing the air clutched at me and caught the fuchsia handkerchief on my wrist. It tore as he went down.

"Then I heard a door bursting open and there was a woman and she looked at me in horror and turned and screamed and ran out and slammed and locked the door.

"And then I realized that I was standing over a dead man with a gun in my hand, and I saw the blood soaking into my slipper. I . . . I lost my head. I just dropped the gun and turned and ran out the French doors. It was a crazy thing to do, I know, but I . . . I . . ."

Inspector Frye nodded understandingly. "But you hadn't planned quite such an emotional climax for your big scene."

"No, not quite."

"But why afterward didn't you come to the police?"

"I was scared. Terribly scared. And everything was so damningly against me. I wasn't even using my own name. I was afraid no one would believe the truth. And then the next day I was . . . he . . ."

"I know," the inspector said. "You were forcibly detained by a young gentleman who was also suffering from a series of misapprehensions."

In the office of the *Gazette*, Lance Sheriton, ace of literary sleuths, was in eclipse and the regular staff had come into its own.

The typewriter of the headquarters man poured forth copy, and at a neighboring desk Miss Doris Deane, the official *Gazette* sob sister, pounded out the beat of the week. Disguising herself as a Bellevue charwoman, she had gotten into Joanna Starr's room and interviewed the girl whose slowly returning consciousness had cleared the shadows from the last dark corners of the Steinmark murder case.

> Two years ago [Doris Deane wrote] Joanna Starr came to New York from Philadelphia. Her parents had died. She had no relatives except a brother who had himself left home years before. He had wanted to be an actor, but his parents had forbidden what they felt was a disgrace to the name of Starr. So he changed it to Saniel and went his own way and eventually landed in Hollywood with a director's job.
>
> In New York, Joanna Starr sought a secretarial career and got a job finally in the office of Jules Konrad, Broad Street attorney. She did not know at the time, of course, that it was the "front" of a notorious gang of which Konrad was the head.

At this point Doris Deane got rather sticky in the manner of sob sisters as she described the process by which the young Joanna, now hopelessly infatuated with Konrad, was separated from her job as secretary and established in the Eighty-seventh Street apartment. With all the trappings. But no publicity. Konrad's visits were so cleverly contrived and so well covered that the attendants at the apartment house had noticed him no more than they would any visitor in a large and busy building.

The copy of the headquarters man continued the story on a less emotional plane.

Careful checking by the police of the confession finally forced from Konrad with the previously known facts of the Newberger kidnaping reveal the following general picture.

Last September the Konrad gang pulled one of its biggest jobs, the kidnaping of young Ronald Newberger from the Newberger estate at Central Islip. It was planned by the very man who stood in closest relation to Charles W. Newberger—his own attorney and confidential adviser, Jules Konrad.

Acting on the direction of the kidnap note, Newberger came to town and procured the $50,000 ransom money. His own town house had not yet been opened for the fall, so he stopped overnight at the Fifty-fourth Street apartment of Konrad. While Konrad went out to buy masculine haberdashery and toilet articles, Newberger prepared the suitcase.

He had brought along with him from Central Islip a heavy brown leather case, a standard style. It's counterpart can be found in almost any household. Jules Konrad happened to have in his apartment a heavy brown leather bag similar to the one which Newberger had brought with him.

Newberger, preoccupied with grief and anxiety, in a moment of abstraction placed the $50,000 ransom money in Konrad's suitcase. But it wasn't really Konrad's suitcase. It belonged to Joanna Starr and he had been using it temporarily. It was marked with her initials.

Neither he nor Newberger noticed the switch at the time, but later the lawyer realized the mistake. Then, however, it was too late. The suitcase was already at the Grand Central checkstand; and

Newberger had already "accidentally" dropped the check at the corner of Broadway and Forty-second, where it had been retrieved by one of Konrad's men stationed there for that purpose.

When Konrad discovered that the suitcases had been mixed by Newberger, he decided to involve the innocent Joanna Starr in such a way that she would unwittingly become part of the kidnap scheme. Accordingly on the following day, pretending great busyness, he asked her to call for the suitcase at Grand Central and take it to her apartment. This she did.

Later, when he found out that Newberger had a memorandum of the serial numbers on the bills, he realized that the $50,000 was "hot money" and would have to be kept "on ice" for a long time, and he reasoned shrewdly that the apartment of the unsuspecting Joanna would be a safe spot.

The headquarters man might have facts as set down in police records and confessions; but Doris Deane had the emotional reactions of Joanna Starr, and she went to town when she got the teeth of her typewriter into the denouement of disillusion that finally forced itself upon the girl.

With the passing months the realization grew upon her that neither Jules Konrad nor her feeling for him was the bright and shining thing she had once thought it. This growing awareness had driven her two months previously to a decision. She must get away for a while to think things over. She started to pack for a brief trip.

She pulled a heavy brown leather suitcase down from its shelf in the closet [Doris Deane continued]. The men's clothes had been removed previously by Konrad. He had made sure—or thought he had—that the bottom lining was smooth and fast. But a pair of manicure scissors, hastily jammed into the case along with other feminine toilet articles, caught on a tiny turned-up corner of the lining that had escaped his notice.

Joanna Starr in removing the scissors peeled back a portion of the lining and revealed one corner of a $500 bill. Her curiosity excited, she wrenched back the rest of the lining and discovered ninety-nine other $500 bills.

Her memory reached back to the time Konrad had borrowed the case and she had retrieved it from the Grand Central checkstand. She remembered, too, that this had occurred about the time when the newspapers had been full of the Newberger kidnaping case. Her suspicions aroused, she consulted back files of the newspapers and copied down the serial numbers and compared them with those on the bills in the suitcase. They were identical.

When she confronted Konrad at last with the irrefutable proof of his complicity in the case, he denied nothing and reminded her that it was *her* suitcase that held the money and that *she* had taken it from Grand Central, and that no court of law would believe that she was anything but an accomplice. This was the hold he had on her and he used it shrewdly to silence her accusations.

The situation was further complicated by the fact that several months previously Trudi Hess, international film star, had decided to find the husband who had deserted her fifteen years before. Her difficulties were confided to Paul Saniel and his advice solicited.

He had not seen his young sister for seven years. When she had first obtained a position as Konrad's secretary she had written him enthusiastic accounts of her employer's brilliance. But later she never confessed to him that she had exchanged her typewriter and independence for the Eighty-seventh Street apartment. He thought she was still "working" for the brilliant lawyer.

It was natural, therefore, that he should recommend Konrad to Trudi Hess as an investigator to trace her husband. He personally had never seen the lawyer, and he made his recommendation solely on the reports of his sister.

Konrad found August Steiner, alias Hugo Steinmark, more than a month ago, but he did not tell Trudi Hess. Steinmark was too rich a plum to surrender.

Faced with blackmail, Steinmark acted on his own. He watched Konrad and trailed him to the Eighty-seventh Street apartment, learned the name of the woman he was visiting. Then secretly he himself visited her.

He was a shrewd judge of human emotion and had once been an actor himself. He soon realized that he was dealing with a woman torn with horrible fears and doubts. He played the role the situation called for with consummate skill—the *deus ex machina*, the kindly stranger from nowhere, bringing promise of strength and protection to one who sought a safe way out of the muddled ruin of her own life. After a series of visits, she broke down and told him everything. He promised her protection and she in turn agreed to deliver the ransom money to him. He wrote her a note telling her when to bring it to his house.

At this point Doris Deane succumbed completely; but her narrative, robbed of sob sister cliché, was, briefly, the story of a girl who, having at last made a decision, found herself smitten with an unreasoning remorse. She had loved Konrad once upon a time and now she was conniving at his betrayal.

She was suddenly overcome with horror and revulsion at herself as well as at him. And to this another emotion was soon added—fear.

In an attempt to break completely with the unfortunate circumstances of her relation with Konrad, she had left the Eighty-seventh Street apartment and gone to a small hotel. But he had found her. She then moved secretly, as she hoped, to a larger one, the Waldorf-Astoria; but she could not shake him off her trail.

She sent a frantic-wire to her brother in Hollywood to come to her; but he had gone on a fishing trip, leaving no address. When she did not hear from him she grew desperate and distrait.

"And so," wrote Doris Deane, "Joanna Starr sought death in a bleak room in a Brooklyn rooming house so that . . ."

Palpitant paragraphs poured from her typewriter and the copy boys snatched it up in short takes and rushed it to the copy desk.

The man from headquarters gathered up loose ends. He wrote:

> Konrad, after ten hours of grilling at the scene of the crime, at last broke and reenacted the murder. On Thursday evening, June 4, he went to Steinmark's house to put on the heat. In the brief interview he had with Steinmark the theatrical producer played his trump card, the Newberger case. Konrad knew then that the game was up.
>
> He left via the front door and drove his car out of the Steinmark driveway and a few hundred feet down Evergreen Drive. Then he returned to the house and hid in the shrubbery flanking the French door at the east end of the library. He knew that it was open because he had left it ajar during his visit, and he knew that Steinmark expected a visit from Joanna Starr. He made his plans accordingly.
>
> . . . figured correctly that in the first burst of panic she would grab the gun, smear it with her fingerprints and . . .
>
> . . . other members of the Konrad gang have already been arrested. One is Max Marten, notorious several years ago in the Skyhigh night club gambling racket. The day Joanna Starr was taken to Bellevue, Marten, under pretext of calling on someone in the

emergency ward, was stationed in the waiting room when Paul Saniel and a woman companion entered.

When Saniel was arrested and the woman immediately afterward tried to see Joanna Starr, posing as a reporter but without a press card, Marten became suspicious and followed her. This was how Konrad knew that she was in the cabin in the Jersey hills. The cabin, which had not been used for several years, was one which had been for a long time the summer vacation camp of the Starr family. Both Joanna Starr and her brother had as children spent . . .

. . . large part of the credit for the solution of the case must go to the man who was first arrested—Paul Saniel. While still in custody he put forward such a brilliant theory of the crime that at last he persuaded the police to let him under the guard of two patrolmen tail Konrad. They arrived at the New Jersey cabin just a few minutes after Konrad had . . .

The hands of the clock in the city room of the *Gazette* moved to eleven . . . eleven-thirty . . .

And farther uptown another clock high on a tower marked the hours and paused. And time waited while a man and a girl looked into each other's eyes across the soft table lights of a garden high among the clouds.

"Coffee?"

"No thanks."

"A liqueur?"

"Yes, please."

"Waiter, two benedictines."

They sipped the heavy sweetness of the liqueur and let the soft night air caress their cheeks and stir faintly the draperies of her gown.

He sighed. "It's such a relief not to have to look at you any more."

"Then why are you doing it?"

"Because now that I don't have to I want to."

"It was your idea originally."

"I know. I thought if I stuck on your trail like grim death I'd find out where Jo was."

"And I thought maybe if I kept still, held tight and didn't speak even when spoken to, I'd find out who you were."

"Pinkey dear, I once called you a fool. Remember?"

She nodded.

"Forgive me, I didn't do you justice. You weren't just a plain fool. You had all the fancy trimmings. You were an outright, goddam fool."

"Yes, I know. Perhaps it was the close association with you. But why didn't you tell me everything that first night?" she demanded.

"I was thinking about Jo. I knew from her telegram she was in some kind of jam, but I didn't know what. Later, after things began to happen, I realized it wasn't just some foolish feminine upset but that in some way she had gotten mixed up with something pretty frightful. I might know she was innocent because she was my own sister and incapable of doing anything really wrong, but the police couldn't be expected to see things that way. So, until I could find out more, I had to walk like a cat on eggs. Why didn't *you* tell *me* all?" His voice was gently accusing.

"Oh, I thought you were part of the jam. Let's dance."

They danced—as if they had danced together all their lives, floating on top of Manhattan as if in some enchanted ship, suspended in the intoxication of space, halfway to heaven.

"Jo's making a wonderful recovery. She wants to see you tomorrow."

She laughed. "To get back her name?"

He grinned. "No, as a matter of fact I think she's rather keen on your keeping it. At least the last half."

"Starr?"

"Pretty name, isn't it? Sorry I had to renounce it, but my parents years ago raised hell. I was so young and so mad at the time that I wrote Jo a note and told her that if she ever told 'em where I was or what name I'd taken I'd—"

"I know. You'd come three thousand miles across the continent and cut her throat."

"How did you know?"

"I found the note, part of it anyway, up there in the cabin—that night."

He sobered. "Don't talk about that night. I almost killed you. I thought you'd killed Jo."

"I was one up on you at that. I thought you'd killed Steinmark and the Newberger child and were *planning* to kill Jo."

"Nice people, weren't we? When did you finally decide I wasn't the villain of the piece?"

"I had my suspicions after we came back to town. Then I was sure that night at Trudi Hess's when you crashed the drawing room conference and dropped a glass and come out looking as if you'd seen a ghost."

"Not a ghost. Konrad. I recognized him as the guy who had trailed you from the Newberger house that morning. I trailed him, you know. Regular procession. All we lacked was a band. You in the lead, then Konrad, then me. Down to the Battery. Konrad was a mug, really. He did too much trailing."

"How do you mean?"

"Well, if he hadn't trailed you down to the Battery I wouldn't have trailed him and got hep to the fact that he was tied in with the Newberger angle of the case. And if he hadn't trailed you out to the cabin, he might still be sitting pretty. There wasn't really anything to tie him to that suitcase. Anything, that is, that would stand up in a court of law. Why were you so keen on getting it?"

"Well, in the first place Jo seemed to think it was awfully important. I suppose she was too upset, her mind was in too much of a turmoil to think logically or rationally about it. She attached undue importance to it because, after all, it was the thing that had tipped her off. It didn't exactly tip me off, but it confirmed a theory I had evolved. I knew that if my theory was correct, that suitcase in the cabin would have all the marks of a ripped up lining. That's what I went out for. For confirmation."

"And Konrad went after you. You know, Pinkey, we weren't the only ones playing tag in the dark. Konrad too. He didn't know how much you knew. He didn't know how much Jo had told you. Maybe she had told you the whole story. In any case, the simplest way out for him was just to ease you out."

"Ease?" A hand touched her throat reminiscently.

"Yeah. That's why he trailed you, and you led him to a spot that was just what the doctor ordered. Nice and quiet and remote. Not like the Battery with a lot of people around."

"And no one to throw him off the trail." She shivered a little. "How did you do it that first time, that day at the Battery?"

"Simple. When you went down into the subway station to get the Bronx express, I got drunk. Stinko."

"I don't understand."

"I reeled into Konrad and fastened myself onto him like a burr and a long-lost brother. You know how drunks are sometimes. I delayed him long enough for you to get a train out. He was mad as hell. He almost called a cop."

She smiled in admiration. "And up there at the Newberger house I thought it was the sight of you across the street that had terrified Jo. But, of course, it was Konrad getting out of the taxi."

"Jumping to false conclusions."

"Yes."

"You did a lot of that, didn't you?"

"What do you mean?"

"Come off it, Pinkey. You know what I mean."

She was flushing and it was very becoming.

"You were jealous of Joanna."

"I wasn't."

"You lie. You were. And of Trudi."

"Now you're being funny."

"No, no. It was you who were funny. That's why I laughed so much sometimes. You thought—"

"Look, you can see the lights of Yonkers from here."

"If you haven't anything better to look at." A smile played about his lips as he watched the deepening flush of her face. "And, anyway, it's White Plains."

"No, White Plains is more to the east. Yonkers is just over there by—"

"Listen, you're getting off the subject."

"What subject?"

"The name of Starr. Legally it's still my name too, you know. Jo wants you to keep it."

For the first time the fluid rhythm of their dancing was broken. She missed a step and his arm tightened around her.

"*Jo* wants me to keep it?" she said. "Jo and who else?"

"Pinkey!" he said. "Pinkey *darling!*"

COACHWHIP PUBLICATIONS
COACHWHIPBOOKS.COM

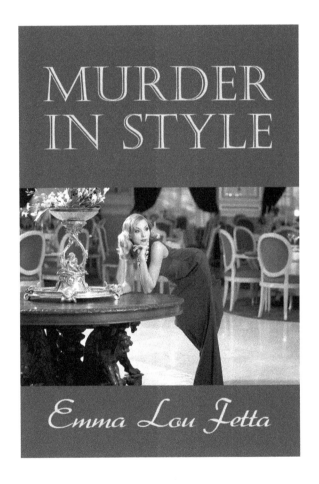

COACHWHIP PUBLICATIONS
CoachwhipBooks.com

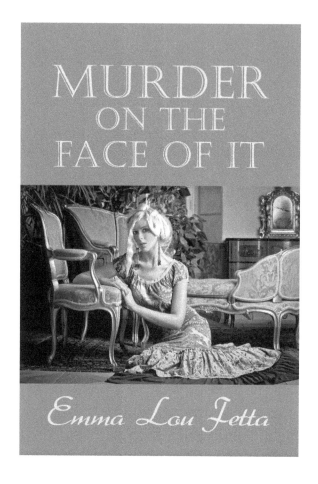

COACHWHIP PUBLICATIONS
CoachwhipBooks.com

COACHWHIP PUBLICATIONS

COACHWHIPBOOKS.COM

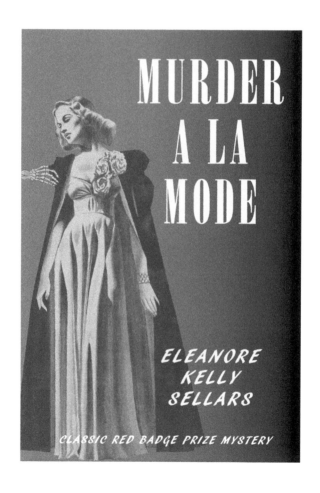

MURDER
A LA
MODE

ELEANORE
KELLY
SELLARS

CLASSIC RED BADGE PRIZE MYSTERY

COACHWHIP PUBLICATIONS
CoachwhipBooks.com

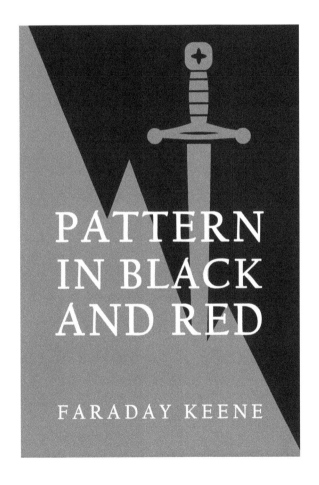

PATTERN
IN BLACK
AND RED

FARADAY KEENE

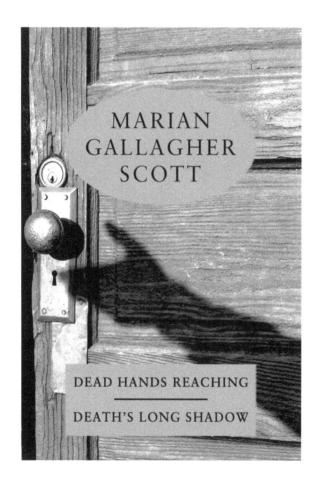

MARIAN
GALLAGHER
SCOTT

DEAD HANDS REACHING

————

DEATH'S LONG SHADOW

COACHWHIP PUBLICATIONS

CoachwhipBooks.com

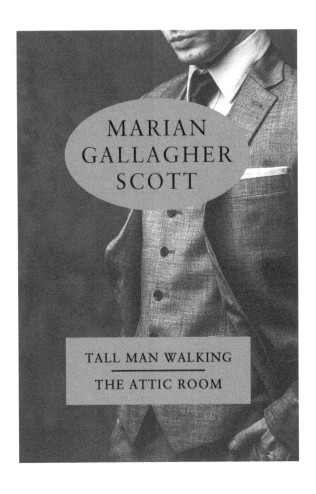

MARIAN
GALLAGHER
SCOTT

TALL MAN WALKING

THE ATTIC ROOM